THE WORKS OF
HENRY VAN DYKE
AVALON EDITION
VOLUME II

ॐ

OUTDOOR ESSAYS
II

From a painting by N.C. Wyeth

The attraction of angling for all the ages
of man,.....lies in its uncertainty. 'Tis
an affair of luck.

FISHERMAN'S LUCK

AND SOME OTHER UNCERTAIN THINGS

BY

HENRY VAN DYKE

"Now I conclude that not only in Physicke, but likewise in
sundry more certaine arts, fortune hath great share in them."
M. DE MONTAIGNE, *Divers Events.*

NEW YORK
CHARLES SCRIBNER'S SONS
1920

DEDICATION

TO MY LADY
GRAYGOWN

HERE
is the basket;
I bring it home to you.
There are no great fish in it.
But perhaps there may be one or two little
ones which will be to your taste. And there
are a few shining pebbles from the bed of the
brook, and ferns from the cool, green woods,
and wild flowers from the places that you remember. I would fain console you, if I could, for
the hardship of having married an angler: a man
who relapses into his mania with the return of
every spring, and never sees a little river without wishing to fish in it. But after all, we have
had good times together as we have followed the
stream of life towards the sea. And we have
passed through the dark days without losing
heart, because we were comrades. So let this
book tell you one thing that is certain.
In all the life of your fisherman
the best piece of luck
is just
YOU.

CONTENTS

FISHERMAN'S LUCK

" She could not conceive a game wanting the sprightly infusion of chance, —the handsome excuses of good fortune."—CHARLES LAMB: *Essays of Elia.*

FISHERMAN'S LUCK

HAVE you ever happened to notice the quality of the greetings that belong to certain occupations?

There is something about these salutations in kind which is singularly taking and grateful to the ear. They are as much better than an ordinary "good day" or a flat "how are you?" as a folk-song of Scotland or the Tyrol is better than the futile love-ditty of the drawing-room. They have a spicy and rememberable flavour. They speak to the imagination and point the way to treasure-trove.

There is a touch of dignity in them, too, for all they are so free and easy—the dignity of independence, the native spirit of one who takes for granted that his mode of living has a right to make its own forms of speech. I admire a man who does not hesitate to salute the world in the dialect of his calling.

How salty and stimulating, for example, is the sailorman's hail of "Ship ahoy!" It is like a breeze laden with briny odours and a pleasant dash of spray. The miners in some parts of

3

FISHERMAN'S LUCK

Germany have a good greeting for their dusky trade. They cry to one who is going down the shaft, *"Glück auf!"* All the perils of an underground adventure and all the joys of seeing the sun again are compressed into a word. Even the trivial salutation which the telephone has lately created and claimed for its peculiar use—"Hello, hello!"—seems to me to have a kind of fitness and fascination. It is like a thoroughbred bulldog, ugly enough to be attractive. There is a lively, concentrated, electric air about it. It makes courtesy wait upon dispatch, and reminds us that we live in an age when it is necessary to be wide awake.

I have often wished that every human employment might evolve its own appropriate greeting. Some of them would be queer, no doubt; but at least they would be an improvement on the wearisome iteration of "Good-evening" and "Good-morning," and the monotonous inquiry, "How do you do?"—a question so conventional that it seldom tarries for an answer. Under the new and more natural system of etiquette, when you passed the time of day with a man you would know his business, and the salutations of the market-place would be full of interest.

As for my chosen pursuit of angling (which I

4

FISHERMAN'S LUCK

follow with diligence when not interrupted by less important concerns), I rejoice with every true fisherman that it has a greeting all its own and of a most honourable antiquity. There is no written record of its origin. But it is quite certain that since the days after the Flood, when Deucalion

> *"Did first this art invent*
> *Of angling, and his people taught the same,"*

two honest and good-natured anglers have never met each other by the way without crying out, "What luck?"

Here, indeed, is an epitome of the gentle art. Here is the spirit of it embodied in a word and paying its respects to you with its native accent. Here you see its secret charm unconsciously disclosed. The attraction of angling for all the ages of man, from the cradle to the grave, lies in its uncertainty. 'Tis an affair of luck.

No amount of preparation in the matter of rods and lines and hooks and lures and nets and creels can change its essential character. No excellence of skill in casting the delusive fly or adjusting the tempting bait upon the hook can make the result secure. You may reduce the chances, but you cannot eliminate them.

5

There are a thousand points at which fortune may intervene. The state of the weather, the height of the water, the appetite of the fish, the presence or absence of other anglers—all these indeterminable elements enter into the reckoning of your success. There is no combination of stars in the firmament by which you can forecast the piscatorial future. When you go a-fishing, you just take your chances; you offer yourself as a candidate for anything that may be going; you try your luck.

There are certain days that are favourites among anglers, who regard them as propitious for the sport. I know a man who believes that the fish always rise better on Sunday than on any other day in the week. He complains bitterly of this supposed fact, because his religious scruples will not allow him to take advantage of it. He confesses that he has sometimes thought seriously of joining the Seventh-Day Baptists.

Among the Pennsylvania Dutch, in the Alleghany Mountains, I have found a curious tradition that Ascension Day is the luckiest in the year for fishing. On that morning the district school is thinly attended, and you must be on the stream very early if you do not wish to find wet footprints on the stones ahead of you.

But in fact, all these superstitions about

fortunate days are idle and presumptuous. If there were such days in the calendar, a kind and firm Providence would never permit the race of man to discover them. It would rob life of one of its principal attractions, and make fishing altogether too easy to be interesting.

Fisherman's luck is so notorious that it has passed into a proverb. But the fault with that familiar saying is that it is too short and too narrow to cover half the variations of the angler's possible experience. For if his luck should be bad, there is no portion of his anatomy, from the crown of his head to the soles of his feet, that may not be thoroughly wet. But if it should be good, he may receive an unearned blessing of abundance not only in his basket, but also in his head and his heart, his memory and his fancy. He may come home from some obscure, ill-named, lovely stream—some Dry Brook, or Southwest Branch of Smith's Run— with a creel full of trout, and a mind full of grateful recollections of flowers that seemed to bloom for his sake, and birds that sang a new, sweet, friendly message to his tired soul. He may climb down to "Tommy's Rock" below the cliffs at Newport (as I have done many a day with my lady Greygown), and, all unnoticed by the idle, weary promenaders in the path of

fashion, haul in a basketful of blackfish, and at
the same time look out across the shining sapphire waters and inherit a wondrous good fortune of dreams—

"Have glimpses that will make him less forlorn;
Have sight of Proteus rising from the sea,
Or hear old Triton blow his wreathèd horn."

But all this, you must remember, depends
upon something secret and incalculable, something that we can neither command nor predict.
It is an affair of gift, not of wages. Fish (and
the other good things which are like sauce to
the catching of them) cast no shadow before.
Water is the emblem of instability. No one
can tell what he shall draw out of it until he
has taken in his line. Herein are found the
true charm and profit of angling for all persons
of a pure and childlike mind.

Look at those two venerable gentlemen floating in a skiff upon the clear waters of Lake
George. One of them is a successful statesman,
an ex-President of the United States, a lawyer
versed in all the curious eccentricities of the
"lawless science of the law." The other is a
learned doctor of medicine, able to give a name
to all diseases from which men have imagined

8

that they suffered, and to invent new ones for those who are tired of vulgar maladies. But all their learning is forgotten, their cares and controversies are laid aside, in "innocuous desuetude." The Summer Schools of Sociology are assembled. The Medical Congresses are in session. But these two men care not—no, not so much as the value of a single live bait. The sun shines upon them with a fervent heat, but it irks them not. The rain descends, and the winds blow and beat upon them, but they are unmoved. They are securely anchored here in the lee of Sabbath-Day Point.

What enchantment binds them to that inconsiderable spot? What magic fixes their eyes upon the point of a fishing-rod, as if it were the finger of destiny? It is the enchantment of uncertainty: the same natural magic that draws the little suburban boys in the spring of the year, with their strings and pin-hooks, around the shallow ponds where dace and red-fins hide; the same irresistible charm that fixes a row of city gamins, like ragged and disreputable fish-crows, on the end of a pier where blear-eyed flounders sometimes lurk in the muddy water. Let the philosopher explain it as he will. Let the moralist reprehend it as he chooses. There is nothing that attracts human

9

nature more powerfully than the sport of tempting the unknown with a fishing-line.

Those ancient anglers have set out upon an
exodus from the tedious realm of the definite,
the fixed, the must-certainly-come-to-pass.
They are on a holiday in the free country of
peradventure. They do not know at this moment whether the next turn of Fortune's reel
will bring up a perch or a pickerel, a sunfish or
a black bass. It may be a hideous catfish or a
squirming eel, or it may be a lake-trout, the
grand prize in the Lake George lottery. There
they sit, those gray-haired lads, full of hope,
yet equally prepared for resignation; taking no
thought for the morrow, and ready to make
the best of to-day; harmless and happy players
at the best of all games of chance.

"In other words," I hear some severe and
sour-complexioned reader say, "in plain language, they are a pair of old gamblers."

Yes, if it pleases you to call honest men by a
bad name. But they risk nothing that is not
their own; and if they lose, they are not im-
poverished. They desire nothing that belongs
to other men; and if they win, no one is robbed.
If all gambling were like that, it would be difficult to see the harm in it. Indeed, a daring
moralist might even assert, and prove by argu-

ment, that so innocent a delight in the taking of chances is an aid to virtue.

Do you remember Martin Luther's reasoning on the subject of "excellent large pike"? He maintains that God would never have created them so good to the taste, if He had not meant them to be eaten. And for the same reason I conclude that this world would never have been left so full of uncertainties, nor human nature framed so as to find a peculiar joy and exhilaration in meeting them bravely and cheerfully, if it had not been divinely intended that most of our amusement and much of our education should come from this source.

"Chance" is a disreputable word, I know. It is supposed by many pious persons to be improper and almost blasphemous to use it. But I am not one of those who share this verbal prejudice. I am inclined rather to believe that it is a good word to which a bad reputation has been given. I feel grateful to that admirable "psychologist who writes like a novelist," Mr. William James, for his brilliant defence of it. For what does it mean, after all, but that some things happen in a certain way which might have happened in another way? Where is the immorality, the irreverence, the atheism in such a supposition? Certainly God must be competent to govern a world in which there are possibilities of various kinds, just as well as one in which every event is inevitably determined beforehand. St. Peter and the other fishermen-disciples on the Lake of Galilee were perfectly free to cast their net on either side of the ship. So far as they could see, so far as any one could see, it was a matter of chance where they chose to cast it. But it was not until they let it down, at the Master's word, on the right side that they had good luck. And not the least element of their joy in the draft of fishes was that it brought a change of fortune.

Leave the metaphysics of the question on the table for the present. As a matter of fact, it is plain that our human nature is adapted to conditions variable, undetermined, and hidden from our view. We are not fitted to live in a world where $a+b$ always equals c, and there is nothing more to follow. The interest of life's equation arrives with the appearance of x, the unknown quantity. A settled, unchangeable, clearly foreseeable order of things does not suit our constitution. It tends to melancholy and a fatty heart. Creatures of habit we are undoubtedly; but it is one of our most fixed habits to be fond of variety. The man who is never surprised does not know the taste of happiness, and un-

12

less the unexpected sometimes happens to us, we are most grievously disappointed.

Much of the tediousness of highly civilized life comes from its smoothness and regularity. To-day is like yesterday, and we think that we can predict to-morrow. Of course we cannot really do so. The chances are still there. But we have covered them up so deeply with the artificialities of life that we lose sight of them. It seems as if everything in our neat little world were arranged, and provided for, and reasonably sure to come to pass. The best way of escape from this *Tædium vitæ* is through a recreation like angling, not only because it is so evidently a matter of luck, but also because it tempts us into a wilder, freer life. It leads almost inevitably to camping out, which is a wholesome and sanitary imprudence.

It is curious and pleasant, to my apprehension, to observe how many people in New England, one of whose States is called "the land of Steady Habits," are sensible of the joy of changing them,—out of doors. These good folk turn out from their comfortable farm-houses and their snug suburban cottages to go a-gypsying for a fortnight among the mountains or beside the sea. You see their white tents gleaming from the pine-groves around the little lakes, and catch glimpses of their bathing-clothes drying in the sun on the wiry grass that fringes the sand-dunes. Happy fugitives from the bondage of routine! They have found out that a long journey is not necessary to a good vacation. You may reach the Forest of Arden in a buckboard. The Fortunate Isles are within sailing distance in a dory. And a voyage on the river Pactolus is open to any one who can paddle a canoe.

I was talking—or rather listening—with a barber, the other day, in the sleepy old town of Rivermouth. He told me, in one of those easy confidences which seem to make the razor run more smoothly, that it had been the custom of his family, for some twenty years past, to forsake their commodious dwelling on Anchor Street every summer, and emigrate six miles, in a wagon to Wallis Sands, where they spent the month of August very merrily under canvas. Here was a sensible household for you! They did not feel bound to waste a year's income on a four weeks' holiday. They were not of those foolish folk who run across the sea, carefully carrying with them the same tiresome mind that worried them at home. They got a change of air by making an alteration of life. They escaped from the Land of Egypt and the

14

House of Bondage by stepping out into the wilderness and going a-fishing.

The people who always live in houses, and sleep on beds, and walk on pavements, and buy their food from butchers and bakers and grocers, are not the most blessed inhabitants of this wide and various earth. The circumstances of their existence are too mathematical and secure for perfect contentment. They live at second or third hand. They are boarders in the world. Everything is done for them by somebody else.

It is almost impossible for anything very interesting to happen to them. They must get their excitement out of the newspapers, reading of the hairbreadth escapes and moving accidents that befall people in real life. What do these tame ducks really know of the adventure of living? If the weather is bad, they are snugly housed. If it is cold, there is a furnace in the cellar. If they are hungry, the shops are near at hand. It is all as dull, flat, stale, and unprofitable as adding up a column of figures. They might as well be brought up in an incubator.

But when man abides in tents, after the manner of the early patriarchs, the face of the world is renewed. The vagaries of the clouds become significant. You watch the sky with a lover's look, eager to know whether it will smile or frown. When you lie at night upon your bed of boughs and hear the rain pattering on the canvas close above your head, you wonder whether it is a long storm or only a shower.

The rising wind shakes the tent-flaps. Are the pegs well driven down and the cords firmly fastened? You fall asleep again and wake later, to hear the rain drumming still more loudly on the tight cloth, and the big breeze snoring through the forest, and the waves plunging along the beach. A stormy day? Well, you must cut plenty of wood and keep the camp-fire glowing, for it will be hard to start it up again, if you let it get too low. There is little use in fishing or hunting in such a storm. But there is plenty to do in the camp: guns to be cleaned, tackle to be put in order, clothes to be mended, a good story of adventure to be read, a belated letter to be written to some poor wretch in a summer hotel, a game of hearts or cribbage to be played, or a hunting-trip to be planned for the return of fair weather. The tent is perfectly dry. A little trench dug around it carries off the surplus water, and luckily it is pitched with the side to the lake, so that you get the pleasant heat of the fire without the unendurable smoke. Cooking in the rain has its disadvantages. But how good the supper tastes when it is served up on a tin plate, with an empty box for a table and a roll of blankets at the foot of the bed for a seat!

A day, two days, three days, the storm may continue, according to your luck. I have been out in the woods for a fortnight without a drop of rain or a sign of dust. Again, I have tented on the shore of a big lake for a week, waiting for an obstinate tempest to pass by.

Look now, just at nightfall: is there not a little lifting and breaking of the clouds in the west, a little shifting of the wind toward a better quarter? You go to bed with cheerful hopes. A dozen times in the darkness you are half awake, and listening drowsily to the sounds of the storm. Are they waxing or waning? Is that louder pattering a new burst of rain, or is it only the plumping of the big drops as they are shaken from the trees? See, the dawn has come, and the gray light glimmers through the canvas. In a little while you will know your fate.

Look! There is a patch of bright yellow radiance on the peak of the tent. The shadow of a leaf dances over it. The sun must be shining. Good luck! and up with you, for it is a glorious morning.

17

FISHERMAN'S LUCK

The woods are glistening as fresh and fair as if they had been new-created overnight. The water sparkles, and tiny waves are dancing and splashing all along the shore. Scarlet berries of the mountain-ash hang around the lake. A pair of kingfishers dart back and forth across the bay, in flashes of living blue. A golden eagle swings silently around his circle, far up in the cloudless sky. The air is full of pleasant sounds, but there is no noise. The world is full of joyful life, but there is no crowd and no confusion. There is no factory chimney to darken the day with its smoke, no trolley-car to split the silence with its shriek and smite the indignant ear with the clanging of its impudent bell. No lumberman's axe has robbed the encircling forests of their glory of great trees. No fires have swept over the hills and left behind them the desolation of a bristly landscape. All is fresh and sweet, calm and clear and bright.

'Twas rather a rude jest of Nature, that tempest of yesterday. But if you have taken it in good part, you are all the more ready for her caressing mood to-day. And now you must be off to get your dinner—not to order it at a shop, but to look for it in the woods and waters. You are ready to do your best with rod or gun. You will use all the skill you have

18

as hunter or fisherman. But what you shall find, and whether you shall subsist on bacon and biscuit, or feast on trout and partridges, is, after all, a matter of luck.

I profess that it appears to me not only pleasant, but also salutary, to be in this condition. It brings us home to the plain realities of life; it teaches us that a man ought to work before he eats; it reminds us that, after he has done all he can, he must still rely upon a mysterious bounty for his daily bread. It says to us, in homely and familiar words, that life was meant to be uncertain, that no man can tell what a day will bring forth, and that it is the part of wisdom to be prepared for disappointments and grateful for all kinds of small mercies.

There is a story in that fragrant book, *The Little Flowers of St. Francis*, which I wish to transcribe here, without tying a moral to it, lest any one should accuse me of preaching.

"Hence [says the quaint old chronicler], having assigned to his companions the other parts of the world, St. Francis, taking Brother Maximus as his comrade, set forth toward the province of France. And coming one day to a certain town, and being very hungry, they begged their bread as they went, according to the rule of their order, for the love of God. And St. Francis went through one quarter of the town, and Brother Maximus through another. But forasmuch as St. Francis was a man mean and low of stature, and hence was reputed a vile beggar by such as knew him not, he only received a few scanty crusts and mouthfuls of dry bread. But to Brother Maximus, who was large and well favoured, were given good pieces and big, and an abundance of bread, yea, whole loaves. Having thus begged, they met together without the town to eat, at a place where there was a clear spring and a fair large stone, upon which each spread forth the gifts that he had received. And St. Francis, seeing that the pieces of bread begged by Brother Maximus were bigger and better than his own, rejoiced greatly, saying, 'Oh, Brother Maximus, we are not worthy of so great a treasure.' As he repeated these words many times, Brother Maximus made answer: 'Father, how can you talk of treasures when there is such great poverty and such lack of all things needful? Here is neither napkin nor knife, neither board nor trencher, neither house nor table, neither man-servant nor maid-servant.' St. Francis replied: 'And this is what I reckon a great treasure, where naught is made ready by human industry,

20

but all that is here is prepared by Divine Providence, as is plainly set forth in the bread which we have begged, in the table of fair stone, and in the spring of clear water. And therefore I would that we should pray to God that He teach us with all our hearts to love the treasure of holy poverty, which is so noble a thing, and whose servant is God the Lord.'"

I know of but one fairer description of a repast in the open air; and that is where we are told how certain poor fishermen, coming in very weary after a night of toil (and one of them very wet after swimming ashore), found their Master standing on the bank of the lake waiting for them. But it seems that he must have been busy in their behalf while he was waiting; for there was a bright fire of coals burning on the shore, and a goodly fish broiling thereon, and bread to eat with it. And when the Master had asked them about their fishing, he said, "Come, now, and take your breakfast." So they sat down around the fire, and with his own hands he served them with the bread and the fish.

Of all the banquets that have ever been given upon earth, that is the one in which I would rather have had a share.

But it is now time that we should return to our fishing. And let us observe with gratitude that almost all of the pleasures that are connected with this pursuit—its accompaniments and variations, which run along with the tune and weave an embroidery of delight around it —have an accidental and gratuitous quality about them. They are not to be counted upon beforehand. They are like something that is thrown into a purchase by a generous and open-handed dealer, to make us pleased with our bargain and inclined to come back to the same shop.

If I knew, for example, before setting out for a day on the brook, precisely what birds I should see, and what pretty little scenes in the drama of woodland life were to be enacted before my eyes, the expedition would lose more than half its charm. But, in fact, it is almost entirely a matter of luck, and that is why it never grows tiresome.

The ornithologist knows pretty well where to look for the birds, and he goes directly to the places where he can find them, and proceeds to study them intelligently and systematically. But the angler who idles down the stream takes them as they come, and all his observations have a flavour of surprise in them.

22

FISHERMAN'S LUCK

He hears a familiar song,—one that he has often heard at a distance, but never identified, —a cheery, rustic cadence sounding from a low pine-tree close beside him. He looks up carefully through the needles and discovers a hooded warbler, a tiny, restless creature, dressed in green and yellow, with two white feathers in its tail, like the ends of a sash, and a glossy little black bonnet drawn closely about its golden head. He will never forget that song again. It will make the woods seem homelike to him, many a time, as he hears it ringing through the afternoon, like the call of a small country girl playing at hide-and-seek: "See *me;* here I *be.*"

Another day he sits down on a mossy log beside a cold, trickling spring to eat his lunch. It has been a barren day for birds. Perhaps he has fallen into the fault of pursuing his sport too intensely, and tramped along the stream looking for nothing but fish. Perhaps this part of the grove has really been deserted by its feathered inhabitants, scared away by a prowling hawk or driven out by nest-hunters. But now, without notice, the luck changes. A surprise-party of redstarts breaks into full play around him. All through the dark-green shadow of the hemlocks they flash like little candles— *candelitas,* the Cubans call them. Their bril-

23

liant markings of orange and black, and their fluttering, airy, graceful movements, make them most welcome visitors. There is no bird in the bush easier to recognize or pleasanter to watch. They run along the branches and dart and tumble through the air in fearless chase of invisible flies and moths. All the time they keep unfolding and furling their rounded tails, spreading them out and waving them and closing them suddenly, just as the Cuban girls manage their fans. In fact, the redstarts are the tiny fantail pigeons of the forest.

There are other things about the birds, beside their musical talents and their good looks, that the fisherman has a chance to observe on his lucky days. He may see something of their courage and their devotion to their young.

I suppose a bird, in spite of its natural timidity, is the bravest creature that lives. From which we may learn that true courage is not incompatible with nervousness, and that heroism does not mean the absence of fear, but the conquest of it. Who does not remember the first time that he ever came upon a hen-partridge with her brood, as he was strolling through the woods in June? How splendidly the old bird forgets herself in her efforts to defend and hide her young!

FISHERMAN'S LUCK

Smaller birds are no less daring. One evening last summer I was walking up the Ristigouche from Camp Harmony to fish for salmon at Mowett's Rock, where my canoe was waiting for me. As I stepped out from a thicket on to the shingly bank of the river, a spotted sandpiper teetered along before me, followed by three young ones. Frightened at first, the mother flew out a few feet over the water. But the piperlings could not fly, having no feathers; and they crept under a crooked log. I rolled the log over very gently and took one of the cowering creatures into my hand—a tiny, palpitating scrap of life, covered with soft gray down, and peeping shrilly, like a Liliputian chicken. And now the mother was transformed. Her fear was changed into fury. She was a bully, a fighter, an Amazon in feathers. She flew at me with loud cries, dashing herself almost into my face. I was a tyrant, a robber, a kidnapper, and she called heaven to witness that she would never give up her offspring without a struggle. Then she changed her tactics and appealed to my baser passions. She fell to the ground and fluttered around me as if her wing were broken. "Look!" she seemed to say, "I am bigger than that poor little baby. If you must eat something, eat me! My wing is lame. I can't fly. You can easily catch me. Let that little bird go!" And so I did; and the whole family disappeared in the bushes as if by magic. I wondered whether the mother was saying to herself, after the manner of her sex, that men are stupid things, after all, and no match for the cleverness of a female who stoops to deception in a righteous cause.

Now, that trivial experience was what I call a piece of good luck—for me, and, in the event, for the sandpiper. But it is doubtful whether it would be quite so fresh and pleasant in the remembrance, if it had not also fallen to my lot to take two uncommonly good salmon on that same evening, in a dry season.

Never believe a fisherman when he tells you that he does not care about the fish he catches. He may say that he angles only for the pleasure of being out-of-doors, and that he is just as well contented when he takes nothing as when he makes a good catch. He may think so, but it is not true. He is not telling a deliberate falsehood. He is only assuming an unconscious pose, and indulging in a delicate bit of self-flattery. Even if it were true, it would not be at all to his credit.

Watch him on that lucky day when he comes home with a full basket of trout on his shoulder, or a quartette of silver salmon covered with green branches in the bottom of the canoe. His face is broader than it was when he went out, and there is a sparkle of triumph in his eye. "It is naught, it is naught," he says, in modest depreciation of his triumph. But you shall see that he lingers fondly about the place where the fish are displayed upon the grass, and does not fail to look carefully at the scales when they are weighed, and has an attentive ear for the comments of admiring spectators. You shall find, moreover, that he is not unwilling to narrate the story of the capture—how the big fish rose short, four times, to four different flies, and finally took a small Black Dose, and played all over the pool, and ran down a terribly stiff rapid to the next pool below, and sulked for twenty minutes, and had to be stirred up with stones, and made such a long fight that, when he came in at last, the hold of the hook was almost worn through, and it fell out of his mouth as he touched the shore. Listen to this tale as it is told, with endless variations, by every man who has brought home a fine fish, and you will perceive that the fisherman does care for his luck, after all.

And why not? I am no friend to the people who receive the bounties of Providence without visible gratitude. When the sixpence falls into your hat, you may laugh. When the messenger of an unexpected blessing takes you by the hand and lifts you up and bids you walk, you may leap and run and sing for joy, even as the lame man, whom St. Peter healed, skipped piously and rejoiced aloud as he passed through the Beautiful Gate of the Temple. There is no virtue in solemn indifference. Joy is just as much a duty as beneficence is. Thankfulness is the other side of mercy.

When you have good luck in anything, you ought to be glad. Indeed, if you are not glad, you are not really lucky.

But boasting and self-glorification I would have excluded, and most of all from the behaviour of the angler. He, more than other men, is dependent for his success upon the favour of an unseen benefactor. Let his skill and industry be never so great, he can do nothing unless *la bonne chance* comes to him.

I was once fishing on a fair little river, the P'tit Saguenay, with two excellent anglers and pleasant companions, H. E. G—— and C. S. D——. They had done all that was humanly possible to secure good sport. The stream had been theoretically protected by a well-paid guardian. The anglers had boxes full of beautiful flies, and casting-lines imported from England, and a rod for every fish in the river. But the weather was "dour," and the water "drumly," and every day the lumbermen sent a "drive" of ten thousand spruce logs rushing down the flooded stream. For three days we had not seen a salmon, and on the fourth, despairing, we went down to angle for sea-trout in the tide of the greater Saguenay. There, in the salt water, where men say the salmon never take the fly, H. E. G——, fishing with a small trout-rod, a poor, short line, and an ancient red ibis of the common kind, rose and hooked a lordly salmon of at least five-and-thirty pounds. Was not this pure luck?

Pride is surely the most unbecoming of all vices in a fisherman. For though intelligence and practice and patience and genius, and many other noble things which modesty forbids him to mention, enter into his pastime, so that it is, as Izaak Walton has firmly maintained, an art; yet, because fortune still plays a controlling hand in the game, its net results should never be spoken of with a haughty and vain spirit. Let not the angler imitate Timoleon, who boasted of his luck and lost it. It is tempting Providence to print the record of your wonderful catches in the sporting newspapers; or at least, if it must be done, there should stand at the head of the column some humble, thankful motto, like "*Non nobis, Domine.*" Even Father Izaak, when he has a fish on his line, says, with a due sense of human limitations, "There is a trout now, and a good one too, *if I can but hold him!*"

This reminds me that we left H. E. G——, a a few sentences back, playing his unexpected salmon, on a trout-rod, in the Saguenay. Four times that great fish leaped into the air; twice he suffered the pliant reed to guide him toward the shore, and twice ran out again to deeper water. Then his spirit awoke within him: he bent the rod like a willow wand, dashed toward the middle of the river, broke the line as if it had been pack-thread, and sailed triumphantly away to join the white whales that were tumbling in the tide. "*Whe-e-ew*," they said, "*whe-e-ew! psha-a-aw!*" blowing out their breath in long, soft sighs as they rolled about like huge snow-balls in the black water. But what did H. E. G—— say? He sat him quietly down upon a rock and reeled in the remnant of his line, uttering these remarkable and Christian words: "Those *marsouins*," said he, "describe the situation rather mildly. But it was good fun while it lasted."

FISHERMAN'S LUCK

Again I remembered a saying of Walton: "Well, Scholar, you must endure worse luck sometimes, or you will never make a good angler."

Or a good man, either, I am sure. For he who knows only how to enjoy, and not to endure, is ill-fitted to go down the stream of life through such a world as this.

I would not have you to suppose, gentle reader, that in discoursing of fisherman's luck I have in mind only those things which may be taken with a hook. It is a parable of human experience. I have been thinking, for instance, of Walton's life as well as of his angling: of the losses and sufferings that he, a firm Royalist, endured when the Commonwealth men came marching into London town; of the consoling days that were granted to him, in troublous times, on the banks of the Lea and the Dove and the New River, and the good friends that he made there, with whom he took sweet counsel in adversity; of the little children who played in his house for a few years, and then were called away into the silent land where he could hear their voices no longer. I was thinking how quietly and peaceably he lived through it all, not complaining nor desponding, but trying to do his work well, whether he was keep-

31

ing a shop or writing books, and seeking to prove himself an honest man and a cheerful companion, and never scorning to take with a thankful heart such small comforts and recreations as came to him.

It is a plain, homely, old-fashioned meditation, reader, but not unprofitable. When I talk to you of fisherman's luck, I do not forget that there are deeper things behind it. I remember that what we call our fortunes, good or ill, are but the wise dealings and distributions of a Wisdom higher, and a Kindness greater, than our own. And I suppose that their meaning is that we should learn, by all the uncertainties of our life, even the smallest, how to be brave and steady and temperate and hopeful, whatever comes, because we believe that behind it all there lies a purpose of good, and over it all there watches a providence of blessing.

In the school of life many branches of knowledge are taught. But the only philosophy that amounts to anything, after all, is just the secret of making friends with our luck.

THE THRILLING MOMENT

"*In angling, as in all other recreations into which excitement enters, we have to be on our guard, so that we can at any moment throw a weight of self-control into the scale against misfortune; and happily we can study to some purpose, both to increase our pleasure in success and to lessen our distress caused by what goes ill. It is not only in cases of great disasters, however, that the angler needs self-control. He is perpetually called upon to use it to withstand small exasperations.*"—SIR EDWARD GREY: *Fly-Fishing.*

THE THRILLING MOMENT

EVERY moment of life, I suppose, is more or less of a turning-point. Opportunities are swarming around us all the time, thicker than gnats at sundown. We walk through a cloud of chances, and if we were always conscious of them they would worry us almost to death.

But happily our sense of uncertainty is soothed and cushioned by habit, so that we can live comfortably with it. Only now and then, by way of special excitement, it starts up wide awake. We perceive how delicately our fortune is poised and balanced on the pivot of a single incident. We get a peep at the oscillating needle, and, because we have happened to see it tremble, we call our experience a crisis.

The meditative angler is not exempt from these sensational periods. There are times when all the uncertainty of his chosen pursuit seems to condense itself into one big chance, and stand out before him like a salmon on the top wave of a rapid. He sees that his luck hangs by a single strand, and he cannot tell whether it will hold or break. This is his thrilling moment, and he never forgets it.

Mine came to me in the autumn of 1894, on the banks of the Unpronounceable River, in the Province of Quebec. It was the last day of the open season for ouananiche, and we had set our hearts on catching some good fish to take home with us. We walked up from the mouth of the river, four preposterously long and rough miles, to the famous fishing-pool, "*la place de pêche à Boivin.*" It was a glorious day for walking; the air was clear and crisp, and all the hills around us were glowing with the crimson foliage of those little bushes which God created to make burned lands look beautiful. The trail ended in a precipitous gully, down which we scrambled with high hopes, and fishing-rods unbroken, only to find that the river was in a condition which made angling absurd if not impossible.

There must have been a cloud-burst among the mountains, for the water was coming down in flood. The stream was bank-full, gurgling and eddying out among the bushes, and rushing over the shoal where the fish used to lie, in a brown torrent ten feet deep. Our last day with the land-locked salmon seemed destined to be a failure, and we must wait eight months

36

before we could have another. There were
three of us in the disappointment, and we
shared it according to our temperaments.

Paul virtuously resolved not to give up while
there was a chance left, and wandered downstream to look for an eddy where he might pick
up a small fish. Ferdinand, our guide, resigned
himself without a sigh to the consolation of eating blueberries, which he always did with great
cheerfulness. But I, being more cast down
than either of my comrades, sought out a convenient seat among the rocks, and, adapting
my anatomy as well as possible to the irregulari-
ties of nature's upholstery, pulled from my
pocket *An Amateur Angler's Days in Dove Dale*,
and settled down to read myself into a Christian frame of mind.

Before beginning, my eyes roved sadly over
the pool once more. It was but a casual glance.
It lasted only for an instant. But in that fortunate fragment of time I distinctly saw the
broad tail of a big ouananiche rise and disappear
in the swift water at the very head of the pool.

Immediately the whole aspect of affairs was
changed. Despondency vanished, and the river
glittered with the beams of rising hope.

Such is the absurd disposition of some anglers.
They never see a fish without believing that

they can catch him; but if they see no fish, they are inclined to think that the river is empty and the world hollow.

I said nothing to my companions. It would have been unkind to disturb them with expectations which might never be realized. My immediate duty was to get within casting distance of that salmon as soon as possible.

The way along the shore of the pool was difficult. The bank was very steep, and the rocks by the river's edge were broken and gliddery. Presently I came to a sheer wall of stone, perhaps thirty feet high, rising directly from the deep water.

There was a tiny ledge or crevice running part of the way across the face of this wall, and by this four-inch path I edged along, holding my rod in one hand, and clinging affectionately with the other to such clumps of grass and little bushes as I could find. There was one small huckleberry plant to which I had a particular attachment. It was fortunately a firm little bush, and as I held fast to it I remembered Tennyson's poem which begins

"Flower in the crannied wall,"

and reflected that if I should succeed in plucking out this flower, "root and all," it would

38

probably result in an even greater increase of knowledge than the poet contemplated.

The ledge in the rock now came to an end. But below me in the pool there was a sunken reef; and on this reef a long log had caught, with one end sticking out of the water, within jumping distance. It was the only chance. To go back would have been dangerous. An angler with a large family dependent upon him for support has no right to incur unnecessary perils.

Besides, the fish was waiting for me at the upper end of the pool!

So I jumped; landed on the end of the log; felt it settle slowly down; ran along it like a small boy on a seesaw, and leaped off into shallow water just as the log rolled from the ledge and lunged out into the stream.

It went wallowing through the pool and down the rapid like a playful hippopotamus. I watched it with interest and congratulated myself that I was no longer embarked upon it. On that craft a voyage down the Unpronounceable River would have been short but far from merry. The "all ashore" bell was not rung soon enough. I just got off, with not half a second to spare.

But now all was well, for I was within reach

of the fish. A little scrambling over the rocks brought me to a point where I could easily cast over him. He was lying in a swift, smooth, narrow channel between two large stones. It was a snug resting-place, and no doubt he would remain there for some time. So I took out my fly-book and prepared to angle for him according to the approved rules of the art.

Nothing is more foolish in sport than the habit of precipitation. And yet it is a fault to which I am singularly subject. As a boy, in Brooklyn, I never came in sight of the Capitoline Skating Pond, after a long ride in the horse-cars, without breaking into a run along the board walk, buckling on my skates in a furious hurry, and flinging myself impetuously upon the ice, as if I feared that it would melt away before I could reach it. Now this, I confess, is a grievous defect, which advancing years have not entirely cured; and I found it necessary to take myself firmly, as it were, by the mental coat-collar, and resolve not to spoil the chance of catching the only ouananiche in the Unpronounceable River by undue haste in fishing for him.

I carefully tested a brand-new leader, and attached it to the line with great deliberation and the proper knot. Then I gave my whole mind to the important question of a wise selection of flies.

It is astonishing how much time and mental anxiety a man can spend on an apparently simple question like this. When you are buying flies in a shop it seems as if you never had half enough. You keep on picking out a half-dozen of each new variety as fast as the enticing salesman shows them to you. You stroll through the streets of Montreal or Quebec and drop in at every fishing-tackle dealer's to see whether you can find a few more good flies. Then, when you come to look over your collection at the critical moment on the bank of a stream, it seems as if you had ten times too many. And, spite of all, the precise fly that you need is not there.

You select a couple that you think fairly good, lay them down beside you in the grass, and go on looking through the book for something better. Failing to satisfy yourself, you turn to pick up those that you have laid out, and find that they have mysteriously vanished from the face of the earth.

Then you struggle with naughty words and relapse into a condition of mental palsy.

Precipitation is a fault. But deliberation, for a person of precipitate disposition, is a vice.

41

FISHERMAN'S LUCK

The best thing to do in such a case is to adopt some abstract theory of action without delay, and put it into practice without hesitation. Then if you fail, you can throw the responsibility on the theory.

Now, in regard to flies there are two theories. The old, conservative theory is, that on a bright day you should use a dark, dull fly, because it is less conspicuous. So I followed that theory first and put on a Great Dun and a Dark Montreal. I cast them delicately over the fish, but he would not look at them.

Then I perverted myself to the new, radical theory which says that on a bright day you must use a light, gay fly, because it is more in harmony with the sky, and therefore less noticeable. Accordingly I put on a Professor and a Parmacheene Belle; but this combination of learning and beauty had no attraction for the ouananiche.

Then I fell back on a theory of my own, to the effect that the ouananiche have an aversion to red, and prefer yellow and brown. So I tried various combinations of flies in which these colours predominated.

Then I abandoned all theories and went straight through my book, trying something from every page, and winding up with that lure

42

which the guides consider infallible,—"a Jock o' Scott that cost fifty cents at Quebec." But it was all in vain. I was ready to despair.

At this psychological moment I heard behind me a voice of hope,—the song of a grasshopper: not one of those fat-legged, green-winged imbeciles that feebly tumble in the summer fields, but a game grasshopper,—one of those thin-shanked, brown-winged fellows that leap like kangaroos, and fly like birds, and sing *Kri-karee-karee-kri* in their flight.

It is not really a song, I know, but it sounds like one; and, if you had heard that Kri-karee carolling as I chased him over the rocks, you would have been sure that he was mocking me.

I believed that he was the predestined lure for that ouananiche; but it was hard to persuade him to fulfill his destiny. I slapped at him with my hat, but he was not there. I grasped at him on the bushes, and brought away "nothing but leaves." At last he made his way to the very edge of the water and poised himself on a stone, with his legs well tucked in for a long leap and a bold flight to the other side of the river. It was my final opportunity. I made a desperate grab at it and caught the grasshopper.

My premonition proved to be correct. When

43

that Kri-karee, invisibly attached to my line, went floating down the stream, the ouananiche was surprised. It was the fourteenth of September, and he had supposed the grasshopper season was over. The unexpected temptation was too strong for him. He rose with a rush, and in an instant I was fast to the best ouananiche of the year.

But the situation was not without its embarrassments. My rod weighed only four and a quarter ounces; the fish weighed between six and seven pounds. The water was furious and headstrong. I had only thirty yards of line and no landing-net.

"*Holà! Ferdinand!*" I cried. "*Apporte la nette, vite! A beauty! Hurry up!*"

I thought it must be an hour while he was making his way over the hill, through the underbrush, around the cliff. Again and again the fish ran out my line almost to the last turn. A dozen times he leaped from the water, shaking his silvery sides. Twice he tried to cut the leader across a sunken ledge. But at last he was played out, and came in quietly towards the point of the rock. At the same moment Ferdinand appeared with the net.

Now, the use of the net is really the most difficult part of angling. And Ferdinand is the

44

best netsman in the Lake St. John country.   He
never makes the mistake of trying to scoop a
fish in motion.   He does not grope around with
aimless, futile strokes as if he were feeling for
something in the dark.   He does not entangle
the dropper-fly in the net and tear the tail-fly
out of the fish's mouth.   He does not get
excited.

He quietly sinks the net in the water, and
waits until he can see the fish distinctly, lying
perfectly still and within reach.   Then he makes
a swift movement, like that of a mower swinging
the scythe, takes the fish into the net head-first,
and lands him without a slip.

I felt sure that Ferdinand was going to do
the trick in precisely this way with my ouananiche.   Just at the right instant he made one
quick, steady swing of the arms, and—the head
of the net broke clean off the handle and went
floating away with the fish in it !

All seemed to be lost.   But Ferdinand was
equal to the occasion.   He seized a long, crooked
stick that lay in a pile of driftwood on the
shore, sprang into the water up to his waist,
caught the net as it drifted past, and dragged
it to land, with the ultimate ouananiche, the
prize of the season, still glittering through its
meshes.

FISHERMAN'S LUCK

This is the story of my most thrilling moment as an angler.

But which was the moment of the deepest thrill?

Was it when the huckleberry bush saved me from a watery grave, or when the log rolled under my feet and started down the river? Was it when the fish rose, or when the net broke, or when the long stick captured it?

No, it was none of these. It was when the Kri-karee sat with his legs tucked under him on the brink of the stream. That was the turning-point. The fortunes of the day depended on the comparative quickness of the reflex action of his neural ganglia and mine. That was the thrilling moment.

I see it now. A crisis is really the commonest thing in the world. The reason why life sometimes seems dull to us is because we do not perceive the importance and the excitement of getting bait.

TALKABILITY

A PRELUDE AND THEME WITH VARIATIONS

"He praises a meditative life, and with evident sincerity : but we feel that he liked nothing so well as good talk."—JAMES RUSSELL LOWELL: *Walton.*

TALKABILITY

I

THE inventor of the familiar maxim that "fishermen must not talk" is lost in the mists of antiquity, and well deserves his fate. For a more foolish rule, a conventionality more obscure and aimless in its tyranny, was never imposed upon an innocent and honourable occupation, to diminish its pleasure and discount its profits. Why, in the name of all that is genial, should anglers go about their harmless sport in stealthy silence like conspirators, or sit together in a boat, dumb, glum, and penitential, like naughty schoolboys on the bench of disgrace? 'Tis an Omorcan superstition; a rule without a reason; a venerable, idiotic fashion invented to repress lively spirits and put a premium on stupidity.

For my part, I incline rather to the opinion of the Neapolitan fishermen who maintain that a certain amount of noise, of certain kinds, is likely to improve the fishing, and who have a particular song, very sweet and charming, which they sing to draw the fishes around them. It is narrated, likewise, of the good St. Brandan, that on his notable voyage from Ireland in search of Paradise, he chanted the service for St. Peter's day so pleasantly that a subaqueous audience of all sorts and sizes was attracted, insomuch that the other monks began to be afraid, and begged the abbot that he would sing a little lower, for they were not quite sure of the intention of the congregation. Of St. Anthony of Padua it is said that he even succeeded in persuading the fishes, in great multitudes, to listen to a sermon; and that when it was ended (it must be noted that it was both short and cheerful) they bowed their heads and moved their bodies up and down with every mark of fondness and approval of what the holy father had spoken.

If we can believe this, surely we need not be incredulous of things which seem to be no less, but rather more, in harmony with the course of nature. Creatures who are sensible to the attractions of a sermon can hardly be indifferent to the charm of other kinds of discourse. I can easily imagine a company of grayling wishing to overhear a conversation between I. W. and his affectionate (but somewhat prodigal) son and follower, Charles Cotton; and surely every intelligent salmon in Scotland might have been glad to hear Christopher North and the Ettrick Shepherd bandy jests and swap stories. As for trout,—was there one in Massachusetts that would not have been curious to listen to the intimate opinions of Daniel Webster as he loafed along the banks of the Marshpee,—or is there one in Pennsylvania to-day that might not be drawn with interest and delight to the feet of Joseph Jefferson, telling how he conceived and wrote *Rip Van Winkle* on the banks of a trout-stream?

Fishermen must be silent? On the contrary, it is far more likely that good talk may promote good fishing.

All this, however, goes upon the assumption that fish can hear, in the proper sense of the word. And this, it must be confessed, is an assumption not yet fully verified. Experienced anglers and students of fishy ways are divided upon the question. It is beyond a doubt that all fishes, except the very lowest forms, have ears. But then so have all men; and yet we have the best authority for believing that there are many who "having ears, hear not."

The ears of fishes, for the most part, are inclosed in their skull, and have no outward opening. Water conveys sound, as every country boy knows who has tried the experiment of diving to the bottom of the swimming-hole and knocking two big stones together. But I doubt whether any country boy, engaged in this interesting scientific experiment, has heard the conversation of his friends on the bank who were engaged in hiding his clothes.

There are many curious and more or less venerable stories to the effect that fishes may be trained to assemble at the ringing of a bell or the beating of a drum. Lucian, a writer of the second century, tells of a certain lake wherein many sacred fishes were kept, of which the largest had names given to them, and came when they were called. But Lucian was not a man of especially good reputation, and there is an air of improbability about his statement that the *largest* fishes came. This is not the custom of the largest fishes.

In the present century there was a tale of an eel in a garden-well, in Scotland, which would come to be fed out of a spoon when the children called him by his singularly inappropriate name of Rob Roy. This seems a more likely story than Lucian's; at all events it comes from a more orthodox atmosphere. But before giving it full credence, I should like to know whether the children, when they called "Rob Roy!" stood where the eel could see the spoon.

On the other side of the question, we may quote Mr. Ronalds, also a Scotchman, and the learned author of *The Fly-Fisher's Entomology*, who conducted a series of experiments which proved that even trout, the most fugacious of fish, are not in the least disturbed by the discharge of a gun, provided the flash is concealed. Mr. Henry P. Wells, the author of *The American Salmon Angler*, says that he has "never been able to make a sound in the air which seemed to produce the slightest effect upon trout in the water."

So the controversy on the hearing of fishes continues, and the conclusion remains open. Every man is at liberty to embrace that side which pleases him best. You may think that the finny tribes are as sensitive to sound as Fine Ear, in the German fairy-tale, who could hear the grass grow. Or you may hold the opposite opinion, that they are

"Deafer than the blue-eyed cat."

But whichever theory you adopt, in practice, if you are a wise fisherman, you will steer a middle course, between one thing which must be left undone and another thing which should be

53

done. You will refrain from stamping on the bank, or knocking on the side of the boat, or dragging the anchor among the stones on the bottom; for when the water vibrates the fish are likely to vanish. But you will indulge as freely as you please in pleasant discourse with your comrade; for it is certain that fishing is never hindered, and may even be helped, in one way or another, by good talk.

I should therefore have no hesitation in advising any one to choose, for companionship on an angling expedition, long or short, a person who has the rare merit of being *talkable*.

II

THEME—ON A SMALL, USEFUL VIRTUE

"Talkable" is not a new adjective. But it needs a new definition, and the complement of a corresponding noun. I would fain set down on paper some observations and reflections which may serve to make its meaning clear, and render due praise to that most excellent quality in man or woman,—especially in anglers,—the small but useful virtue of *talkability*.

Robert Louis Stevenson uses the word "talkable" in one of his essays to denote a certain distinction among the possible subjects of human speech. There are some things, he says in effect, about which you can really talk; and there are other things about which you cannot properly talk at all, but only dispute, or harangue, or prose, or moralize, or chatter.

After mature consideration I have arrived at the opinion that this distinction among the themes of speech is an illusion. It does not exist. All subjects, "the foolish things of the world, and the weak things of the world, and base things of the world, yea, and things that are not," may provide matter for good talk, if only the right people are engaged in the enterprise. I know a man who can make a description of the weather as entertaining as a tune on the violin; and even on the threadbare theme of the waywardness of domestic servants, I have heard a discreet woman play the most diverting and instructive variations.

No, the quality of talkability does not mark a distinction among things; it denotes a difference among people. It is not an attribute unequally distributed among material objects and abstract ideas. It is a virtue which belongs to the mind and moral character of certain persons. It is a reciprocal human quality; active as well as passive; a power of bestowing and receiving.

An amiable person is one who has a capacity

for loving and being loved. An affable person is one who is ready to speak and to be spoken to,—as, for example, Milton's "affable arch-angel" Raphael; though it must be confessed that he laid the chief emphasis on the active side of his affability. A "clubbable" person (to use a word which Dr. Samuel Johnson invented but did not put into his dictionary) is one who is fit for the familiar give and take of club-life. A talkable person, therefore, is one whose nature and disposition invite the easy interchange of thoughts and feelings, one in whose company it is a pleasure to talk or to be talked to.

Now this good quality of talkability is to be distinguished, very strictly and inflexibly, from the bad quality which imitates it and often brings it into discredit. I mean the vice of talkativeness. That is a selfish, one-sided, inharmonious affair, full of discomfort, and productive of most unchristian feelings.

You may observe the operations of this vice not only in human beings, but also in birds. All the birds in the bush can make some kind of a noise; and most of them like to do it; and some of them like it a great deal and do it very much. But it is not always for edification, nor are the most vociferous and garrulous birds

56

commonly the most pleasing. A parrot, for instance, in your neighbour's back yard, in the summer time, when the windows are open, is not an aid to the development of Christian character. I knew a man who had to stay in the city all summer, and in the autumn was asked to describe the character and social standing of a new family that had moved into his neighbourhood. Were they "nice people," well-bred, intelligent, respectable? "Well," said he, "I don't know what your standards are, and would prefer not to say anything libellous; but I'll tell you in a word,—they are the kind of people that keep a parrot."

Then there is the English Sparrow! What an insufferable chatterbox, what an incurable scold, what a voluble and tiresome blackguard is this little feathered cockney. There is not a sweet or pleasant word in all his vocabulary.

I am convinced that he talks altogether of scandals and fights and street-sweepings.

The kingdom of ornithology is divided into two departments,—real birds and English sparrows. English sparrows are not real birds; they are little beasts.

There was a church in Brooklyn which was once covered with a great and spreading vine, in which the sparrows built innumerable nests.

These ungodly little birds kept up such a din that it was impossible to hear the service of the sanctuary. The faithful clergy strained their voices to the verge of ministerial sore throat, but the people had no peace in their devotions until the vine was cut down, and the Anglican intruders were evicted.

A talkative person is like an English sparrow, —a bird that cannot sing, and will sing, and ought to be persuaded not to try to sing. But a talkable person has the gift that belongs to the wood thrush and the veery and the wren, the oriole and the white-throat and the rose-breasted grosbeak, the mockingbird and the robin (sometimes); and the brown thrasher; yes, the brown thrasher has it to perfection, if you can catch him alone,—the gift of being interesting, charming, delightful, in the most off-hand and various modes of utterance.

Talkability is not at all the same thing as eloquence. The eloquent man surprises, overwhelms, and sometimes paralyzes us by the display of his power. Great orators are seldom good talkers. Oratory in exercise is masterful and jealous, and intolerant of all interruptions. Oratory in preparation is silent, self-centred, uncommunicative. The painful truth of this remark may be seen in the row of countenances along the president's table at a public banquet

58

about nine o'clock in the evening. The bicycle-face seems unconstrained and merry by comparison with the after-dinner-speech-face. The flow of table-talk is corked by the anxious conception of post-prandial oratory.

Thackeray, in one of his *Roundabout Papers*, speaks of "the sin of tall-talking," which, he says, "is the sin of schoolmasters, governesses, critics, sermoners, and instructors of young or old people." But this is not in accord with my observation. I should say it was rather the sin of dilettanti who are ambitious of that high-stepping accomplishment which is called "conversational ability."

This has usually, to my mind, something set and artificial about it, although in its most perfect form the art almost succeeds in concealing itself. But, at all events, "conversation" is talk in evening dress, with perhaps a little powder and a touch of rouge. 'T is like one of those wise virgins who are said to look their best by lamplight. And doubtless this is an excellent thing, and not without its advantages. But for my part, commend me to one who loses nothing by the early morning illumination,—one who brings all her attractions with her when she comes down to breakfast,—she is a very pleasant maid.

Talk is that form of human speech which is

exempt from all duties, foreign and domestic. It is the nearest thing in the world to thinking and feeling aloud. It is necessarily not for publication,—solely an evidence of good faith and mutual kindness. You tell me what you have seen and what you are thinking about, because you take it for granted that it will interest and entertain me; and you listen to my replies and the recital of my adventures and opinions, because you know I like to tell them, and because you find something in them, of one kind or another, that you care to hear. It is a nice game, with easy, simple rules, and endless possibilities of variation. And if we go into it with the right spirit, and play it for love, without heavy stakes, the chances are that if we happen to be fairly talkable people we shall have one of the best things in the world,—a mighty good talk.

What is there in this anxious, hide-bound, tiresome existence of ours, more restful and remunerative? Montaigne says, "The use of it is more sweet than of any other action of life; and for that reason it is that, if I were compelled to choose, I should sooner, I think, consent to lose my sight than my hearing and speech." The very aimlessness with which it proceeds, the serene disregard of all considerations of profit and propriety with which it follows its wandering course, and brings up anywhere or nowhere, to camp for the night, is one of its attractions. It is like a day's fishing, not valuable *chiefly* for the fish you bring home, but for the pleasant country through which it leads you, and the state of personal well-being and health in which it leaves you, warmed, and cheered, and content with life and friendship.

The order in which you set out upon a talk, the path which you pursue, the rules which you observe or disregard, make but little difference in the end. You may follow the advice of Immanuel Kant if you like, and begin with the weather and the roads, and go on to current events, and wind up with history, art, and philosophy. Or you may reverse the order if you prefer, like that admirable talker Clarence King, who usually set sail on some highly abstract paradox, such as "Civilization is a nervous disease," and landed in a tale of adventure in Mexico or the Rocky Mountains. Or you may follow the example of Edward Eggleston, who started in at the middle and worked out at either end, and sometimes at both. It makes no difference. If the thing is in you at all, you will find good matter for talk anywhere along the route. Hear what Montaigne says again:

"In our discourse all subjects are alike to me; let there be neither weight nor depth, 't is all one; there is yet grace and pertinence; all there is tinted with a mature and constant judgment, and mixed with goodness, freedom, gaiety, and friendship."

How close to the mark the old essayist sends his arrow! He is right about the essential qualities of good talk. They are not merely intellectual. They are moral. Goodness of heart, freedom of spirit, gaiety of temper, and friendliness of disposition,—these are four fine things, and doubtless as acceptable to God as they are agreeable to men. The talkability which springs out of these qualities has its roots in a good soil. On such a plant one need not look for the poison berries of malign discourse, nor for the Dead Sea apples of frivolous mockery. But fair fruit will be there, pleasant to the sight and good for food, brought forth abundantly according to the season.

TALKABILITY

III

Montaigne has given us our text, "Goodness, freedom, gaiety, and friendship,"—these are the conditions which produce talkability. And on this fourfold theme we may embroider a few variations, by way of exposition and enlargement.

Goodness is the first thing and the most needful. An ugly, envious, irritable disposition is not fitted for talk. The occasions for offence are too numerous, and the way into strife is too short and easy. A touch of good-natured combativeness, a fondness for brisk argument, a readiness to try a friendly bout with any comer, on any ground, is a decided advantage in a talker. It breaks up the offensive monotony of polite concurrence, and makes things lively. But quarrelsomeness is quite another affair, and very fatal.

I am always a little uneasy in a discourse with Bellicosus Macduff. It is like playing golf on links liable to earthquakes. One never knows when the landscape will be thrown into convulsions. Macduff has a tendency to regard a

63

difference of opinion as a personal insult. If he makes a bad stroke he seems to think that the way to retrieve it is to deliver the next one on the head of the other player. He does not tarry for the invitation to lay on; and before you know what has happened you find yourself in a position where you are obliged to cry, "Hold, enough!" and to be liberally damned without any bargain to that effect. This is discouraging, and calculated to make one wish that human intercourse might be put, as far as Macduff is concerned, upon the gold basis of silence.

On the other hand, what a delight it was to talk with that old worthy, Doctor Howard Crosby! He was a fighting man for four or five generations back, Dutch on one side, English on the other. But there was not one little drop of gall in his blood. His opinions were fixed to a degree; he loved to do battle for them; he never changed them—at least never in the course of the same discussion. He admired and respected a gallant adversary, and urged him on, with quips and puns and daring assaults and unqualified statements, to do his best. Easy victories were not to his taste. Even if he joined with you in laying out some common falsehood for burial, you might be sure that be-

64

fore the affair was concluded there would be every prospect of what an Irishman would call "an elegant wake." If you stood up against him on one of his favorite subjects of discussion you must be prepared for hot work. You would have to take off your coat. But when the combat was over he would be the man to help you on with it again; and you would walk home together arm in arm, through the twilight, smoking the pipe of peace. Talk like that does good. It quickens the beating of the heart, and leaves no scars upon it.

But this manly spirit, which loves

"To drink delight of battle with its peers,"

is a very different thing from that mean, bad, hostile temper which loves to inflict wounds and injuries just for the sake of showing power, and which is never so happy as when it is making some one wince. There are such people in the world, and sometimes their brilliancy tempts us to forget their malignancy. But to have much converse with them is as if we should make playmates of rattlesnakes for their grace of movement and swiftness of stroke.

I knew a man once (I will not name him even with an initial) who was malignant to the core. Learned, industrious, accomplished, he kept all

65

his talents at the service of a perfect genius for hatred. If you crossed his path but once, he would never cease to curse you. The grave might close over you, but he would revile your epitaph and mock at your memory. It was not even necessary that you should do anything to incur his enmity. It was enough to be upright and sincere and successful, to waken the wrath of this Shimei. Integrity was an offence to him, and excellence of any kind filled him with spleen. There was no good cause within his horizon that he did not give a bad word to, and no decent man in the community whom he did not try either to use or to abuse. To listen to him or to read what he had written was to learn to think a little worse of every one that he mentioned, and worst of all of him. He had the air of a gentleman, the vocabulary of a scholar, the style of a Junius, and the heart of a Thersites.

Talk, in such company, is impossible. The sense of something evil, lurking beneath the play of wit, is like the knowledge that there are snakes in the grass. Every step must be taken with fear. But the real pleasure of a walk through the meadow comes from the feeling of security, of ease, of safe and happy abandon to the mood of the moment. This ungirdled and unguarded felicity in mutual discourse depends, after all, upon the assurance of real goodness in your companion. I do not mean a stiff impeccability of conduct. Prudes and Pharisees are poor comrades. I mean simply goodness of heart, the wholesome, generous, kindly quality which thinketh no evil, rejoiceth not in iniquity, hopeth all things, endureth all things, and wisheth well to all men. Where you feel this quality you can let yourself go, in the ease of hearty talk.

Freedom is the second note that Montaigne strikes, and it is essential to the harmony of talking. Very careful, prudent, precise persons are seldom entertaining in familiar speech. They are like tennis players in too fine clothes. They think more of their costume than of the game.

A mania for absolutely correct pronunciation is fatal. The people who are afflicted with this painful ailment are as anxious about their utterance as dyspeptics about their diet. They move through their sentences as delicately as Agag walked. Their little airs of nicety, their starched cadences and frilled phrases seem as if they had just been taken out of a literary bandbox. If perchance you happen to misplace an accent, you shall see their eyebrows

67

curl up like an interrogation mark, and they will ask you what authority you have for that pronunciation. As if, forsooth, a man could not talk without book-license! As if he must have a permit from some dusty lexicon before he can take a good word into his mouth and speak it out like the people with whom he has lived!

The truth is that the man who is very particular not to commit himself, in pronunciation or otherwise, and talks as if his remarks were being taken down in shorthand, and shudders at the thought of making a mistake, will hardly be able to open your heart or let out the best that is in his own.

Reserve and precision are a great protection to overrated reputations; but they are death to talk.

In talk it is not correctness of grammar nor elegance of enunciation that charms us; it is spirit, *verve*, the sudden turn of humour, the keen, pungent taste of life. For this reason a touch of dialect, a flavour of brogue, is delightful. Any dialect is classic that has conveyed beautiful thoughts. Who that ever talked with the poet Tennyson, when he let himself go, over the pipes, would miss the savour of his broadrolling Lincolnshire vowels, now heightening the humour, now deepening the pathos, of his genuine manly speech? There are many good stories lingering in the memories of those who knew Dr. James McCosh, the late president of Princeton University,—stories too good, I fear, to get into a biography; but the best of them, in print, would not have the snap and vigour of the poorest of them, in talk, with his own inimitable Scotch-Irish brogue to set it forth.

A brogue is not a fault. It is a beauty, an heirloom, a distinction. A local accent is like a landed inheritance; it marks a man's place in the world, tells where he comes from. Of course it is possible to have too much of it. A man does not need to carry the soil of his whole farm around with him on his boots. But, within limits, the accent of a native region is delightful. 'T is the flavour of heather in the grouse, the taste of wild herbs and evergreen-buds in the venison. I like the maple-sugar tang of the Vermonter's sharp-edged speech; the round, full-waisted r's of Pennsylvania and Ohio; the soft, indolent vowels of the South. One of the best talkers now living is an ex-schoolmaster from Virginia, Colonel Gordon McCabe. I once crossed the ocean with him on a stream of stories that reached from Liverpool to New York. He did not talk in the least like a book. He talked like a Virginian.

FISHERMAN'S LUCK

When Montaigne mentions *gaiety* as the third element of satisfying discourse, I fancy he does not mean mere fun, though that has its value at the right time and place. But there is another quality which is far more valuable and always fit. Indeed it underlies the best fun and makes it wholesome. It is cheerfulness, the temper which makes the best of things and gets the little drops of honey even out of thistle-blossoms. I think this is what Montaigne meant. Certainly it is what he had.

Cheerfulness is the background of all good talk. A sense of humour is a means of grace. With it I have heard a pleasant soul make even that most perilous of all subjects, the description of a long illness, entertaining. The various physicians moved through the recital as excellent comedians, and the medicines appeared like a succession of timely jests.

There is no occasion upon which this precious element of talkability comes out stronger than when we are on a journey. Travel with a cheerless and easily discouraged companion is an unadulterated misery. But a cheerful comrade is better than a waterproof coat and a foot-warmer.

I remember riding once with my lady Gray-gown fifteen miles through a cold rainstorm, in

TALKABILITY

an open buckboard, over the worst road in the world, from *Lac à la Belle Rivière* to the Metabetchouan River. Such was the cheerfulness of her ejaculations (the only possible form of talk) that we arrived at our destination as warm and merry as if we had been sitting beside a roaring camp-fire.

But after all, the very best thing in good talk, and the thing that helps it most, is *friendship*. How it dissolves the barriers that divide us, and loosens all constraint, and diffuses itself like some fine old cordial through all the veins of life—this feeling that we understand and trust each other, and wish each other heartily well! Everything into which it really comes is good. It transforms letter-writing from a task into a pleasure. It makes music a thousand times more sweet. The people who play and sing not *at* us, but *to* us,—how delightful it is to listen to them! Yes, there is a talkability that can express itself even without words. There is an exchange of thought and feeling which is happy alike in speech and in silence. It is quietness pervaded with friendship.

Having come thus far in the exposition of Montaigne, I shall conclude with an opinion of

71

my own, even though I cannot quote a sentence of his to back it.

The one person of all the world in whom talk-ability is most desirable, and talkativeness least endurable, is a wife.

A WILD STRAWBERRY

"*Such is the story of the Boblink; once spiritual, musical, admired, the joy of the meadows, and the favourite bird of spring; finally a gross little sensualist who expiates his sensuality in the larder. His story contains a moral, worthy the attention of all little birds and little boys; warning them to keep to those refined and intellectual pursuits which raised him to so high a pitch of popularity during the early part of his career; but to eschew all tendency to that gross and dissipated indulgence, which brought this mistaken little bird to an untimely end.*"—WASHINGTON IRVING: *Wolfert's Roost.*

A WILD STRAWBERRY

THE Swiftwater brook was laughing softly to itself as it ran through a strip of hemlock forest on the edge of the Woodlings' farm. Among the evergreen branches overhead the gayly-dressed warblers,—little friends of the forest,—were flitting to and fro, lisping their June songs of contented love: milder, slower, lazier notes than those in which they voiced the amorous raptures of May. Prince's Pine and golden loose-strife and pink laurel and blue hare-bells and purple-fringed orchids, and a score of lovely flowers were all abloom. The late spring had hindered some; the sudden heats of early summer had hastened others; and now they seemed to come out all together, as if Nature had suddenly tilted up her cornucopia and poured forth her treasures in spendthrift joy.

I lay on a mossy bank at the foot of a tree, filling my pipe after a frugal lunch, and thinking how hard it would be to find in any quarter of the globe a place more fair and fragrant than this hidden vale among the Alleghany Mountains. The perfume of the flowers of the northern forest is more sweet and subtle than the heavy scent of tropical blossoms. No lily-field in Bermuda could give a fragrance half so magical as the fairy-like odour of these woodland slopes, soft carpeted with the green of glossy vines above whose tiny leaves, in delicate profusion,

"The slight Linnæa *hangs its twin-born heads."*

Nor are there any birds in Africa, or among the Indian Isles, more exquisite in colour than these miniature warblers, showing their gold and green, their orange and black, their blue and white, against the dark background of the rhododendron thicket.

But how seldom we put a cup of pleasure to our lips without a dash of bitters, a touch of faultfinding. My drop of discontent, that day, was the thought that the northern woodland, at least in June, yielded no fruit to match its beauty and its fragrance.

There is good browsing among the leaves of the wood and the grasses of the meadow, as every well-instructed angler knows. The bright emerald tips that break from the hemlock and the balsam like verdant flames have a pleasant savour to the tongue. The leaves of the sassafras are full of spice, and the bark of the black-birch twigs holds a fine cordial. Crinkle-root is spicy, but you must partake of it delicately, or it will bite your tongue. Spearmint and peppermint never lose their charm for the palate that still remembers the delights of youth. Wild sorrel has an agreeable, sour, shivery flavour. Even the tender stalk of a young blade of grass is a thing that can be chewed by a person of childlike mind with much contentment.

But, after all, these are only relishes. They whet the appetite more than they appease it. There should be something to eat, in the June woods, as perfect in its kind, as satisfying to the sense of taste, as the birds and the flowers are to the senses of sight and hearing and smell. Blueberries are good, but they are far away in August. Blackberries are luscious when fully ripe, but that will not be until September. Then the fishing will be over, and the angler's hour of need will be past. The one thing that is lacking now beside this mountain stream is some fruit more luscious and dainty than grows in the tropics, to melt upon the lips and fill the mouth with pleasure.

But that is what these cold northern woods will not offer. They are too reserved, too lofty, too puritanical to make provision for the grosser wants of humanity. They are not friendly to luxury.

Just then, as I shifted my head to find a softer pillow of moss after this philosophic and immoral reflection, Nature gave me her silent answer. Three wild strawberries, nodding on their long stems, hung over my face. It was an invitation to taste and see that they were good.

The berries were not the round and rosy ones of the meadow, but the long, slender, dark crimson ones of the forest. One, two, three; no more on that vine; but each one as it touched my lips was a drop of nectar and a crumb of ambrosia, a concentrated essence of all the pungent sweetness of the wildwood, sapid, penetrating, and delicious. I tasted the odour of a hundred blossoms and the green shimmering of innumerable leaves and the sparkle of sifted sunbeams and the breath of highland breezes and the song of many birds and the murmur of flowing streams,—all in a wild strawberry.

Do you remember, in *The Compleat Angler*, a remark which Izaak Walton quotes from a certain "Doctor Boteler" about strawberries? "*Doubtless*," said that wise old man, "*God could have made a better berry, but doubtless God never did.*"

A WILD STRAWBERRY

Well, the wild strawberry is the one that God made.

I think it would have been pleasant to know a man who could sum up his reflections upon the important question of berries in such a pithy saying as that which Walton repeats. His tongue must have been in close communication with his heart. He must have had a fair sense of that sprightly humour without which piety itself is often insipid.

I have often tried to find out more about him, and some day I hope I shall. But up to the present, all that the books have told me of this obscure sage is that his name was William Butler, and that he was an eminent physician, sometimes called "the Æsculapius of his age." He was born at Ipswich, in 1535, and educated at Clare Hall, Cambridge; in the neighbourhood of which town he appears to have spent the most of his life, in high repute as a practitioner of physic. He had the honour of doctoring King James the First after an accident on the hunting field, and must have proved himself a pleasant fellow, for the king looked him up at Cambridge the next year, and spent an hour in his lodgings. This wise physician also invented a medicinal beverage called "Doctor Butler's Ale." I do not quite like the sound of it, but perhaps it was better than its name. This much is sure, at all events: either it was really a harmless drink, or else the doctor must have confined its use entirely to his patients; for he lived to the ripe age of eighty-three years.

Between the time when William Butler first needed the services of a physician, in 1535, and the time when he last prescribed for a patient, in 1618, there was plenty of trouble in England. Bloody Queen Mary sat on the throne; and there were all kinds of quarrels about religion and politics; and Catholics and Protestants were killing one another in the name of God. After that the red-haired Elizabeth, called the Virgin Queen, wore the crown, and waged triumphant war and tempestuous love. Then fat James of Scotland was made king of Great Britain; and Guy Fawkes tried to blow him up with gunpowder, and failed; and the king tried to blow out all the pipes in England with his *Counterblast Against Tobacco;* but he failed too. Somewhere about that time, early in the seventeenth century, a very small event happened. A new berry was brought over from Virginia, —*Fragraria Virginiana*,—and then, amid wars and rumours of wars, Doctor Butler's happiness was secure. That new berry was so much richer and sweeter and more generous than the familiar

A WILD STRAWBERRY

Fragraria vesca of Europe, that it attracted the sincere interest of all persons of good taste. It inaugurated a new era in the history of the strawberry. The long lost masterpiece of Paradise was restored to its true place in the affections of man.

Is there not a touch of merry contempt for all the vain controversies and conflicts of humanity in the grateful ejaculation with which the old doctor greeted that peaceful, comforting gift of Providence?

"From this time forward," he seems to say, "the fates cannot beggar me, for I have eaten strawberries. With every Maytime that visits this distracted island, the white blossoms with hearts of gold will arrive. In every June the red drops of pleasant savour will hang among the scalloped leaves. The children of this world may wrangle and give one another wounds that even my good ale cannot cure. Nevertheless, the earth as God created it is a fair dwelling and full of comfort for all who have a quiet mind and a thankful heart. Doubtless God might have made a better world, but doubtless this is the world He made for us; and in it He planted the strawberry."

Fine old doctor! Brave philosopher of cheerfulness! The Virginian berry should have been brought to England sooner, or you should have lived longer, at least to a hundred years, so that you might have welcomed a score of strawberry-seasons with gratitude and an epigram.

Since that time a great change has passed over the fruit which Doctor Butler praised so well. That product of creative art which Divine wisdom did not choose to surpass, human industry has laboured to improve. It has grown immensely in size and substance. The traveller from America who steams into Queenstown harbour in early summer is presented (for a consideration) with a cabbage-leaf full of pale-hued berries, sweet and juicy, any one of which would outbulk a dozen of those that used to grow in Virginia when Pocahontas was smitten with the charms of Captain John Smith. They are superb, those light-tinted Irish strawberries. And there are wonderful new varieties developed in the gardens of New Jersey and Rhode Island, which compare with the ancient berries of the woods and meadows as Leviathan with a minnow. The huge crimson cushions hang among the plants so thick that they seem like bunches of fruit with a few leaves attached for ornament. You can satisfy your hunger in such a berry-patch in ten minutes, while out in the field you must pick for half an hour, and in the

A WILD STRAWBERRY

forest thrice as long, before you can fill a small tin cup.

Yet, after all, it is questionable whether men have really bettered God's *chef d'œuvre* in the berry line. They have enlarged it and made it more plentiful and more certain in its harvest. But sweeter, more fragrant, more poignant in its flavour? No. The wild berry still stands first in its subtle gusto.

Size is not the measure of excellence. Perfection lies in quality, not in quantity. Concentration enhances pleasure, gives it a point so that it goes deeper.

Is not a ten-inch trout better than a ten-foot sturgeon? I would rather read a tiny essay by Charles Lamb than a five-hundred page libel on life by a modern British novelist who shall be nameless. Flavour is the priceless quality. Style is the thing that counts and is remembered, in literature, in art, and in berries.

No *Jocunda*, nor *Triumph*, nor *Victoria*, nor any other high-titled fruit that ever took the first prize at an agricultural fair, is half so delicate and satisfying as the wild strawberry that dropped into my mouth, under the hemlock tree, beside the Swiftwater.

A touch of surprise is essential to perfect sweetness.

83

FISHERMAN'S LUCK

To get what you have been wishing for is pleasant; but to get what you have not been sure of, makes the pleasure tingle. A new door of happiness is opened when you go out to hunt for something and discover it with your own eyes. But there is an experience even better than that. When you have stupidly forgotten (or despondently foregone) to look about you for the unclaimed treasures and unearned blessings which are scattered along the by-ways of life, then, sometimes by a special mercy, a small sample of them is quietly laid before you so that you cannot help seeing it, and it brings you back to a sense of the joyful possibilities of living.

How full of enjoyment is the search after wild things,—wild birds, wild flowers, wild honey, wild berries! There was a country club on Storm King Mountain, above the Hudson River, where they used to celebrate a festival of flowers every spring. Men and women who had conservatories of their own, full of rare plants and costly orchids, came together to admire the gathered blossoms of the woodlands and meadows. But the people who had the best of the entertainment were the boys and girls who wandered through the thickets and down the brooks, pushed their way into the tangled

copses and crept venturesomely across the
swamps, to look for the flowers. Some of the
seekers may have had a few gray hairs; but for
that day at least they were all boys and girls.
Nature was as young as ever, and they were all
her children. Hand touched hand without a
glove. The hidden blossoms of friendship un-
folded. Laughter and merry shouts and snatches
of half-forgotten song rose to the lips. Gay adventure sparkled in the air. School was out
and nobody listened for the bell. It was just
a day to live, and be natural, and take no
thought for the morrow.

There is great luck in this affair of looking for
flowers. I do not see how any one who is prej-
udiced against games of chance can consistently
undertake it.

For my own part, I approve of garden flowers
because they are so orderly and so certain; but
wild flowers I love, just because there is so
much chance about them. Nature is all in
favour of certainty in great laws and of uncertainty in small events. You cannot appoint
the day and the place for her flower-shows. If
you happen to drop in at the right moment she
will give you a free admission. But even then
it seems as if the table of beauty had been
spread for the joy of a higher visitor, and in

obedience to secret orders which you have not heard.

Have you ever found the fringed gentian?

> *"Just before the snows,*
> *There came a purple creature*
> *That lavished all the hill;*
> *And summer hid her forehead,*
> *And mockery was still.*
>
> *The frosts were her condition:*
> *The Tyrian would not come*
> *Until the North evoked her,—*
> *'Creator, shall I bloom?'"*

There are strange freaks of fortune in the finding of wild flowers, and curious coincidences which make us feel as if some one were playing friendly tricks on us. I remember reading, one evening in May, a passage in a good book called *The Procession of the Flowers*, in which Colonel Higginson describes the singular luck that a friend of his enjoyed, year after year, in finding the rare blossoms of the double rue-anemone. It seems that this man needed only to take a walk in the suburbs of any town, and he would come upon a bed of these flowers, without effort or design. I envied him his good fortune, for

86

A WILD STRAWBERRY

I had never discovered even one of them. But the next morning, as I strolled out to fish the Swiftwater, down below Billy Lerns's spring-house I found a green bank in the shadow of the wood all bespangled with tiny, trembling, two-fold stars,—double rue-anemones, for luck! It was a favourable omen, and that day I came home with a creel full of trout.

The theory that Adam lived out in the woods for some time before he was put into the garden of Eden "to dress it and to keep it" has an air of probability. How else shall we account for the arboreal instincts that cling to his posterity?

There is a wilding strain in our blood that all the civilization in the world will not eradicate. I never knew a real boy—or, for that matter, a girl worth knowing—who would not rather climb a tree, any day, than walk up a golden stairway.

It is a touch of this instinct, I suppose, that makes it more delightful to fish in the most insignificant of free streams than in a carefully stocked and preserved pond, where the fish are brought up by hand and fed on minced liver. Such elaborate precautions to ensure good luck extract all the spice from the sport of angling. Casting the fly in such a pond, if you hooked a fish, you might expect to hear the keeper say, "Ah, that is Charles, we will play him and put him back, if you please, sir; for the master is very fond of him,"—or, "Now you have got hold of Edward; let us land him and keep him; he is three years old this month, and just ready to be eaten." It would seem like taking trout out of cold storage.

Who could find any pleasure in angling for the tame carp in the fish-pool of Fontainebleau? They gather at the marble steps, those venerable, courtly fish, to receive their rations; and there are veterans among them, in ancient livery, with fringes of green moss on their shoulders, who could tell you pretty tales of being fed by the white hands of maids of honour, or even of nibbling their crumbs of bread from the jewelled fingers of a princess.

There is no sport in bringing pets to the table. It may be necessary sometimes; but the true sportsman would always prefer to leave the unpleasant task of execution to menial hands, while he goes out into the wild country to capture his game by his own skill,—if he has good luck. I would rather run some risk in this enterprise (even as the young Tobias did, when the voracious pike sprang at him from the waters of the Tigris, and would have devoured

him but for the friendly instruction of the piscatory Angel, who taught Tobias how to land
the monster),—I would far rather take any
number of chances in my sport than have it
domesticated to the point of dulness.

The trim plantations of trees which are called
"forests" in certain parts of Europe—scien-
tifically pruned and tended, counted every year
by uniformed foresters, and defended against all
possible depredations—are admirable and useful in their way; but they lack the mystic enchantment of the fragments of native woodland which linger among the Adirondacks and
the White Mountains, or the vast, shaggy, sylvan
wildernesses which hide the lakes and rivers of
Canada. These Laurentian Hills lie in No
Man's Land. Here you do not need to keep to
the path, for there is none. You may make
your own trail, whithersoever fancy leads you;
and at night you may pitch your tent under any
tree that looks friendly and firm.

Here, if anywhere, you shall find Dryads, and
Naiads, and Oreads. And if you chance to see
one, by moonlight, combing her long hair beside the glimmering waterfall, or slipping silently,
with gleaming shoulders, through the grove of
silver birches, you may call her by the name
that pleases you best. She is all your own dis-

covery. There is no social directory in the wilderness.

One side of our nature, no doubt, finds its satisfaction in the regular, the proper, the conventional. But there is another side of our nature, underneath, that takes delight in the strange, the free, the spontaneous. We like to discover what we call a law of Nature, and make our calculations about it, and harness the force which lies behind it for our own purposes. But we taste a different kind of joy when an event occurs which nobody has foreseen or counted upon. It seems like an evidence that there is something in the world which is alive and mysterious and untrammelled.

The weather-prophet tells us of an approaching storm. It comes according to the programme. We admire the accuracy of the prediction, and congratulate ourselves that we have such a good meteorological service. But when, perchance, a bright, crystalline piece of weather arrives instead of the foretold tempest, do we not feel a secret sense of pleasure which goes beyond our mere comfort in the sunshine? The whole affair is not as easy as a sum in simple addition, after all,—at least not with our present knowledge. It is a good joke on the

A WILD STRAWBERRY

Weather Bureau. "Aha, Old Probabilities!" we say, "you don't know it all yet; there are still some chances to be taken!"

Some day, I suppose, all things in the heavens above, and in the earth beneath, and in the hearts of the men and women who dwell between, will be investigated and explained. We shall live a perfectly ordered life, with no accidents, happy or unhappy. Everybody will act according to rule, and there will be no dotted lines on the map of human existence, no regions marked "unexplored." Perhaps that golden age of the machine will come, but you and I will hardly live to see it. And if that seems to you a matter for tears, you must do your own weeping, for I cannot find it in my heart to add a single drop of regret.

The results of education and social discipline in humanity are fine. It is a good thing that we can count upon them. But at the same time let us rejoice in the play of native traits and individual vagaries. Cultivated manners are admirable, yet there is a sudden touch of inborn grace and courtesy that goes beyond them all. No array of accomplishments can rival the charm of an unsuspected gift of nature, brought suddenly to light. I once heard a peasant girl singing down the Traunthal, and the echo of her song outlives, in the hearing of my heart, all memories of the grand opera.

The harvest of the gardens and the orchards, the result of prudent planting and patient cultivation, is full of satisfaction. We anticipate it in due season, and when it comes we fill our mouths and are grateful. But pray, kind Providence, let me slip over the fence out of the garden now and then, to shake a nut-tree that grows untended in the wood. Give me liberty to put off my black coat for a day, and go a-fishing on a free stream, and find by chance a wild strawberry.

LOVERS AND LANDSCAPE

"*He insisted that the love that was of real value in the world was n't interesting, and that the love that was interesting was n't always admirable. Love that happened to a person like the measles or fits, and was really of no particular credit to itself or its victims, was the sort that got into the books and was made much of; whereas the kind that was attained by the endeavour of true souls, and that had wear in it, and that made things go right instead of tangling them up, was too much like duty to make satisfactory reading for people of sentiment.*"—E. S. MARTIN: *My Cousin Anthony.*

LOVERS AND LANDSCAPE

THE first day of spring is one thing, and the first spring day is another. The difference between them is sometimes as great as a month.

The first day of spring is due to arrive, if the calendar does not break down, about the twenty-first of March, when the earth turns the corner of Sun Alley and starts for Summer Street. But the first spring day is not on the time-table at all. It comes when it is ready, and in the latitude of New York this is usually not till after All Fools' Day.

About this time,—

> "*When chinks in April's windy dome*
> *Let through a day of June,*
> *And foot and thought incline to roam,*
> *And every sound's a tune,*"—

it is the habit of the angler who lives in town to prepare for the labours of the approaching season by longer walks or bicycle-rides in the parks, or along the riverside, or in the somewhat de-moralized Edens of the suburbs. In the course of these vernal peregrinations and circumrotations, I observe that lovers of various kinds begin to occupy a notable place in the landscape.

The burnished dove puts a livelier iris around his neck, and practises fantastic bows and amorous quicksteps along the verandah of the pigeon-house and on every convenient roof. The young male of the human species, less gifted in the matter of rainbows, does his best with a gay cravat, and turns the thoughts which circulate above it towards the securing or propitiating of a best girl.

The objects of these more or less brilliant attentions, doves and girls, show a becoming reciprocity, and act in a way which leads us to infer (so far as inferences hold good in the mysterious region of female conduct) that they are not seriously displeased. To a rightly tempered mind, pleasure is a pleasant sight. And the philosophic observer who could look upon this spring spectacle of the lovers with any but friendly feelings would be indeed what the great Dr. Samuel Johnson called "a person not to be envied."

Far be it from me to fall into such a desiccated and supercilious mood. My small olive-branch of fancy will be withered, in truth, and ready to drop budless from the tree, when I cease to feel a mild delight in the billings and cooings of the little birds that separate from the flocks to fly together in pairs, or in the uninstructive but mutually satisfactory converse which Strephon holds with Chloe while they dally along the primrose path.

I am glad that even the stony and tumultuous city affords some opportunities for these amiable observations. In the month of April there is hardly a clump of shrubbery in the Central Park which will not serve as a trysting-place for yellow warblers and catbirds just home from their southern tours. At the same time, you shall see many a bench, designed for the accommodation of six persons, occupied at the sunset hour by only two, and apparently so much too small for them that they cannot avoid a little crowding.

These are infallible signs. Taken in conjunction with the eruption of tops and marbles among the small boys, and the purchase of fishing-tackle and golf-clubs by the old boys, they certify us that the vernal season has arrived, not only in the celestial regions, but also in the heart of man.

I have been reflecting of late upon the relation of lovers to the landscape, and questioning whether art has given it quite the same place as that which belongs to it in nature. In fiction, for example, and in the drama, and in music, I have some vague misgivings that romantic love has come to hold a more prominent and a more permanent position than it fills in real life.

This is dangerous ground to venture upon, even in the most modest and deprecatory way. The man who expresses an opinion, or even a doubt, on this subject, contrary to the ruling traditions, will have a swarm of angry critics buzzing about him. He will be called a heretic, a heathen, a cold-blooded freak of nature. As for the woman who hesitates to subscribe all the thirty-nine articles of romantic love, if such a one dares to put her reluctance into words, she is certain to be accused either of unwomanly ambition or of feminine disappointment.

Let us make haste, then, to get back for safety to the ornithological aspect of the subject. Here there can be no penalties for heresy. And here I make bold to avow my conviction that the pairing season is not the only point of interest in the life of the birds; nor is the instinct by which they mate altogether and beyond comparison the noblest passion that stirs their feathered breasts.

'T is true, the time of mating is their prettiest

98

season; but it is very short. How little we should know of the drama of their airy life if we had eyes only for this brief scene! Their finest qualities come out in the patient cares that protect the young in the nest, in the varied struggles for existence through the changing year, and in the incredible heroisms of the annual migrations. Herein is a parable.

It may be observed further, without fear of rebuke, that the behaviour of the different kinds of birds during the prevalence of romantic love is not always equally above reproach. The courtship of English sparrows—blustering, noisy, vulgar—is a sight to offend the taste of every gentle on-looker. Some birds reiterate and vociferate their love-songs in a fashion that displays their inconsiderateness as well as their ignorance of music. This trait is most marked in domestic fowls. There was a guinea-cock, once, that chose to do his wooing close under the window of a farm-house where I was lodged. He had no regard for my hours of sleep or meditation. His amatory click-clack prevented the morning and wrecked the tranquillity of the evening. It was odious, brutal,—worse, it was absolutely thoughtless. Herein is another parable.

Let us admit cheerfully that lovers have a

99

place in the landscape and lend a charm to it. This does not mean that they are to take up all the room there is. Suppose, for example, that a pair of them, on Goat Island, put themselves in such a position as to completely block out your view of Niagara. You cannot regard them with gratitude. They even become a little tedious. Or suppose that you are visiting at a country-house, and you find that you must not enjoy the moonlight on the verandah because Augustus and Amanda are murmuring in one corner, and that you must not go into the garden because Louis and Lizzie are there, and that you cannot have a sail on the lake because Richard and Rebecca have taken the boat.

Of course, unless you happen to be a selfish old curmudgeon, you rejoice, by sympathy, in the happiness of these estimable young people. But you fail to see why it should cover so much ground.

Why should they not pool their interests, and all go out in the boat, or all walk in the garden, or all sit on the verandah? Then there would be room for somebody else about the place.

In old times you could rely upon lovers for retirement. But nowadays their rôle seems to be a bold ostentation of their condition. They rely upon other people to do the timid, shrinking part. Society, in America, is arranged principally for their convenience; and whatever portion of the landscape strikes their fancy, they preëmpt and occupy. All this goes upon the presumption that romantic love is really the only important interest in life.

This train of thought was illuminated, the other night, by an incident which befell me at a party. It was an assembly of men, drawn together by their common devotion to the sport of canoeing. There were only three or four of the gentler sex present (as honorary members), and only one of whom it could be suspected that she was at that time a victim or an object of the tender passion. In the course of the evening, by way of diversion to our disputations on keels and centreboards, canvas and birch-bark, cedar-wood and bass-wood, paddles and steering-gear, a fine young Apollo, with a big, manly voice, sang us a few songs. But he did not chant the joys of weathering a sudden squall, or running a rapid feather-white with foam, or floating down a long, quiet, elm-bowered river. Not he! His songs were full of sighs and yearnings, languid lips and sheep's-eyes. His powerful voice informed us that crowns of thorns seemed like garlands of roses, and kisses were as sweet as samples of heaven, and various other curious sensations were experienced; and at the end of every stanza the reason was stated, in tones of thunder—

"Because I love you, dear."

Even if true, it seemed inappropriate. How foolish the average audience in a drawing-room looks while it is listening to passionate love-ditties! And yet I suppose the singer chose these songs, not from any malice aforethought, but simply because songs of this kind are so abundant that it is next to impossible to find anything else in the shops.

In regard to novels, the situation is almost as discouraging. Ten love-stories are printed to one of any other kind. We have a standing invitation to consider the tribulations and difficulties of some young man or young woman in finding a mate. It must be admitted that the subject has its capabilities of interest. Nature has her uses for the romantic lover, and she gives him an excellent part to play in the drama of life. But is this tantamount to saying that his interest is perennial and all-absorbing, and that his rôle on the stage is the only one that is significant and noteworthy?

Life is much too large to be expressed in the terms of a single passion. Friendship, patriotism, parental tenderness, filial devotion, the ardour of adventure, the thirst for knowledge, the ecstasy of religion,—these all have their dwelling in the heart of man. They mould character. They control conduct. They are stars of destiny shining in the inner firmament. And if art would truly hold the mirror up to nature, it must reflect these greater and lesser lights that rule the day and the night.

How many of the plays that divert and misinform the modern theatre-goer turn on the pivot of a love-affair, not always pure, but generally simple! And how many of those that are imported (or imitated) from France proceed upon the theory that the Seventh is the only Commandment, and that the principal attraction of life lies in the opportunity of breaking it! The matinée-girl is not likely to have a very luminous or truthful idea of existence floating around in her pretty little head.

But, after all, the great plays, those that take the deepest hold upon the heart, like *Hamlet* and *King Lear*, *Macbeth* and *Othello*, are not love-plays. And the most charming comedies, like *The Winter's Tale*, and *The Rivals*, and *Rip Van Winkle*, are chiefly memorable for other things than love-scenes.

Even in novels, love shows at its best when it

does not absorb the whole plot. *Lorna Doone* is a lovers' story, but there is a blessed minimum of spooning in it, and always enough of working and fighting to keep the air clear and fresh. *The Heart of Midlothian*, and *Hypatia*, and *Romola*, and *The Cloister and the Hearth*, and *John Inglesant*, and *The Three Musketeers*, and *Nôtre Dame*, and *Peace and War*, and *Quo Vadis*,—these are great novels because they are much more than tales of romantic love. As for *Henry Esmond*, (which seems to me the best of all,) certainly "love at first sight" does not play the finest rôle in that book.

There are good stories of our own day—pathetic, humourous, entertaining, powerful—in which the element of romantic love is altogether subordinate, or even imperceptible. *The Rise of Silas Lapham* does not owe its deep interest to the engagement of the very charming young people who enliven it. *Madame Delphine* and *Ole 'Stracted* are perfect stories of their kind. I would not barter *The Jungle Books* for a hundred of *The Brushwood Boy*.

The truth is that love, considered merely as the preference of one person for another of the opposite sex, is not "the greatest thing in the world." It becomes great only when it leads on, as it often does, to heroism and self-sacrifice and fidelity. Its chief value for art (the interpreter) lies not in itself, but in its quickening relation to the other elements of life. It must be seen and shown in its due proportion, and in harmony with the broader landscape.

Do you believe that in all the world there is only one woman specially created for each man, and that the order of the universe will be hopelessly askew unless these two needles find each other in the haystack? You believe it for yourself, perhaps; but do you believe it for Tom Johnson? You remember what a terrific disturbance he made in the summer of 189–, at Bar Harbor, about Ellinor Brown, and how he ran away with her in September. You have also seen them together (occasionally) at Lenox and Newport, since their marriage. Are you honestly of the opinion that if Tom had not married Ellinor, these two young lives would have been a total wreck?

Adam Smith, in his book on *The Moral Sentiments*, goes so far as to say that "love is not interesting to the observer because it is *an affection of the imagination*, into which it is difficult for a third party to enter." Something of the same kind occurred to me in regard to

105

Tom and Ellinor. Yet I would not have presumed to suggest this thought to either of them. Nor would I have quoted in their hearing the melancholy and frigid prediction of Ralph Waldo Emerson, to the effect that they would some day discover "that all which at first drew them together—those once sacred features, that magical play of charm—was deciduous."

Deciduous, indeed? Cold, unpleasant, botanical word! Rather would I prognosticate for the lovers something perennial,

"A sober certainty of waking bliss,"

to survive the evanescence of love's young dream. Ellinor should turn out to be a woman like the Lady Elizabeth Hastings, of whom Richard Steele wrote that "to love her was a liberal education." Tom should prove that he had in him the lasting stuff of a true man and a hero. Then it would make little difference whether their conjunction had been eternally prescribed in the book of fate or not. It would be evidently a fit match, made on earth and illustrative of heaven.

But even in the making of such a match as this, the various stages of attraction, infatuation, and appropriation should not be displayed

106

too prominently before the world, nor treated as events of overwhelming importance and enduring moment. I would not counsel Tom and Ellinor, in the mid-summer of their engagement, to have their photographs taken together in affectionate attitudes.

The pictures of an imaginary kind which deal with the subject of romantic love are, almost without exception, fatuous and futile. The inanely amatory, with their languishing eyes, weary us. The endlessly osculatory, with their protracted salutations, are sickening. Even when an air of sentimental propriety is thrown about them by some such title as "Wedded" or "The Honeymoon," they fatigue us. For the most part, they remind me of the remark which the Commodore made upon a certain painting of Jupiter and Io which used to hang in the writing-room of the Contrary Club, but has now been retired to the upper stairway.

"Sir," said that gently piercing critic, "that picture is equally unsatisfactory to the artist, to the moralist, and to the voluptuary."

Nevertheless, having made a clean breast of my misgivings and reservations on the subject of lovers and landscape, I will now confess

107

that the whole of my doubts do not weigh much against my unreasoned faith in romantic love. At heart I am no infidel, but a most obstinate believer and devotee. My seasons of skepticism are transient. They are connected with a torpid liver and aggravated by confinement to a sedentary life and enforced abstinence from angling. Out-of-doors, I return to a saner and happier frame of mind.

As my wheel rolls along the Riverside Drive in the golden glow of the sunset, I rejoice that the episode of Charles Henry and Matilda Jane has not been omitted from the view. This vast and populous city, with all its passing show of life, would be little better than a waste, howling wilderness if we could not catch a glimpse, now and then, of young people falling in love in the good old-fashioned way. Even on a trout-stream, I have seen nothing prettier than the sight upon which I once came suddenly as I was fishing down the Neversink.

A boy was kneeling beside the brook, and a girl was giving him a drink of water out of her rosy hands. They stared with wonder and compassion at the wet and solitary angler, wading down the stream, as if he were some kind of a mild lunatic. But as I glanced discreetly at their small tableau, I was not uncon-

scious of the new joy that came into the landscape with the presence of

"A lover and his lass."

I knew how sweet the water tasted from that
kind of a cup. I also have lived in Arcadia,
and have not forgotten the way back.

A FATAL SUCCESS

"What surprises me in her behaviour," said he, *"is its thoroughness. Woman seldom does things by halves, but often by doubles."*—SOLOMON SINGLEWITZ: *The Life of Adam.*

A FATAL SUCCESS

BEEKMAN DE PEYSTER was probably
the most passionate and triumphant fisherman in the Petrine Club. He angled with the
same dash and confidence that he threw into
his operations in the stock-market. He was
sure to be the first man to get his flies on the
water at the opening of the season. And when
we came together for our fall meeting, to compare notes of our wanderings on various streams
and make up the fish-stories for the year, Beekman was almost always "high hook." We ex-
pected, as a matter of course, to hear that he
had taken the most and the largest fish.

It was so with everything that he undertook.
He was a masterful man. If there was an un-
usually large trout in a river, Beekman knew
about it before any one else, and got there first,
and came home with the fish. It did not make
him unduly proud, because there was nothing
uncommon about it. It was his habit to succeed, and all the rest of us were hardened to it.

When he married Cornelia Cochrane, we
were consoled for our partial loss by the appar-

113

ent fitness and brilliancy of the match. If Beekman was a masterful man, Cornelia was certainly what you might call a mistressful woman. She had been the head of her house since she was eighteen years old. She carried her good looks like the family plate; and when she came into the breakfast-room and said good-morning, it was with an air as if she presented every one with a check for a thousand dollars. Her tastes were accepted as judgments, and her preferences had the force of laws. Wherever she wanted ·to go in the summertime, there the finger of household destiny pointed. At Newport, at Bar Harbor, at Lenox, at Southampton, she made a record. When she was joined in holy wedlock to Beekman De Peyster, her father and mother heaved a sigh of satisfaction, and settled down for a quiet vacation in Cherry Valley.

It was in the second summer after the wedding that Beekman admitted to a few of his ancient Petrine cronies, in moments of confidence (unjustifiable, but natural), that his wife had one fault.

"It is not exactly a fault," he said, "not a positive fault, you know. It is just a kind of a defect, due to her education, of course. In everything else she's magnificent. But she

114

does n't care for fishing. She says it 's stupid, —can't see why any one should like the woods, —calls camping out the lunatic's diversion. It 's rather awkward for a man with my habits to have his wife take such a view. But it can be changed by training. I intend to educate her and convert her. I shall make an angler of her yet."

And so he did.

The new education was begun in the Adirondacks, and the first lesson was given at Paul Smith's. It was a complete failure.

Beekman persuaded her to come out with him for a day on Meacham River, and promised to convince her of the charm of angling. She wore a new sporting-gown, fawn-colour and violet, with a picture-hat, very taking. But the Meacham River trout was shy that day; not even Beekman could induce him to rise to the fly. What the trout lacked in confidence the mosquitoes more than made up. Mrs. De Peyster came home much sunburned, and expressed a highly unfavourable opinion of fishing as an amusement and of Meacham River as a resort.

"The nice people don't come to the Adirondacks to fish," said she; "they come to talk about the fishing twenty years ago. Besides, what do you want to catch that trout for? If you do, the other men will say you bought it, and the hotel will have to put in a new one for the rest of the season."

The following year Beekman tried Moose-head Lake. Here he found an atmosphere more favourable to his plan of education. There were a good many people who really fished, and short expeditions in the woods were quite fashiona-ble. Cornelia had a camping-costume of the most approved style made by Dewlap on Fifth Avenue,—pearl-gray with linings of rose-silk, —and consented to go with her husband on a trip up Moose River. They pitched their tent the first evening at the mouth of Misery Stream, and a storm came on. The rain sifted through the canvas in a fine spray, and Mrs. De Peyster sat up all night in a waterproof cloak, holding an umbrella. The next day they were back at the hotel in time for lunch.

"It was horrid," she told her most intimate friend, "perfectly horrid. The idea of sleeping in a shower-bath, and eating your breakfast from a tin plate, just for sake of catching a few silly fish! Why not send your guides out to get them for you?"

But, in spite of this profession of obstinate heresy, Beekman observed with secret joy that there were signs, before the end of the season,

that Cornelia was drifting a little, a very little
but still perceptibly, in the direction of a change
of heart. She began to take an interest, as the
big trout came along in September, in the re-
ports of the catches made by the different
anglers. She would saunter out with the other
people to the corner of the porch to see the fish
weighed and spread out on the grass. Several
times she went with Beekman in the canoe to
Hardscrabble Point, and showed distinct evi-
dences of pleasure when he caught large trout.
The last day of the season, when he returned
from a successful expedition to Roach River
and Lily Bay, she inquired with some partic-
ularity about the results of his sport; and in
the evening, as the company sat before the great
open fire in the hall of the hotel, she was heard
to use this information with considerable skill
in putting down Mrs. Minot Peabody of Boston, who was recounting the details of her
husband's catch at Spencer Pond. Cornelia
was not a person to be contented with the back
seat, even in fish-stories.

When Beekman observed these indications
he was much encouraged, and resolved to push
his educational experiment briskly forward to
his customary goal of success.

"Some things can be done, as well as others,"

he said in his masterful way, as three of us were walking home together after the autumnal dinner of the Petrine Club, which he always attended as a graduate member. "A real fisherman never gives up. I told you I'd make an angler out of my wife; and so I will. It has been rather difficult. She is 'dour' in rising. But she's beginning to take notice of the fly now. Give me another season, and I'll have her landed."

Good old Beekman! Little did he think— But I must not interrupt the story with moral reflections.

The preparations that he made for his final effort at conversion were thorough and prudent. He had a private interview with Dewlap in regard to the construction of a practical fishing-costume for a lady, which resulted in something more reasonable and workmanlike than had ever been turned out by that famous artist. He ordered from Hook & Catchett a lady's angling-outfit of the most enticing description, —a split-bamboo rod, light as a girl's wish, and strong as a matron's will; an oxidized silver reel, with a monogram on one side, and a sapphire set in the handle for good luck; a book of flies, of all sizes and colours, with the correct names inscribed in gilt letters on each page. He surrounded his favourite sport with an aureole of elegance and beauty. And then he took Cornelia in September to the Upper Dam at Rangeley.

She went reluctant. She arrived disgusted. She stayed incredulous. She returned— Wait a bit, and you shall hear how she returned.

The Upper Dam at Rangeley is the place, of all others in the world, where the lunacy of angling may be seen in its incurable stage. There is a cosy little inn, called a camp, at the foot of a big lake. In front of the inn is a huge dam of gray stone, over which the river plunges into a great oval pool, where the trout assemble in the early fall to perpetuate their race. From the tenth of September to the thirtieth, there is not an hour of the day or night when there are no boats floating on that pool, and no anglers trailing the fly across its waters. Before the late fishermen are ready to come in at midnight, the early fishermen may be seen creeping down to the shore with lanterns in order to begin before cock-crow. The number of fish taken is not large,—perhaps five or six for the whole company on an average day,— but the size is sometimes enormous,—nothing under three pounds is counted,—and they pervade thought and conversation at the Upper

119

Dam to the exclusion of every other subject. There is no driving, no dancing, no golf, no tennis. There is nothing to do but fish or die.

At first, Cornelia thought she would choose the latter alternative. But a remark of that skilful and morose old angler, McTurk, which she overheard on the verandah after supper, changed her mind.

"Women have no sporting instinct," said he. "They only fish because they see men doing it. They are imitative animals."

That same night she told Beekman, in the subdued tone which the architectural construction of the house imposes upon all confidential communications in the bedrooms, but with resolution in every accent, that she proposed to go fishing with him on the morrow.

"But not on that pool, right in front of the house, you understand. There must be some other place, out on the lake, where we can fish for three or four days, until I get the trick of this wobbly rod. Then I'll show that old bear, McTurk, what kind of an animal woman is."

Beekman was simply delighted. Five days of diligent practice at the mouth of Mill Brook brought his pupil to the point where he pronounced her safe.

A FATAL SUCCESS

"Of course," he said patronizingly, "you have n't learned all about it yet. That will take years. But you can get your fly out thirty feet, and you can keep the tip of your rod up. If you do that, the trout will hook himself, in rapid water, eight times out of ten. For playing him, if you follow my directions, you 'll be all right. We will try the pool to-night, and hope for a medium-sized fish."

Cornelia said nothing, but smiled and nodded. She had her own thoughts.

At about nine o'clock Saturday night, they anchored their boat on the edge of the shoal where the big eddy swings around, extinguished the lantern and began to fish. Beekman sat in the bow of the boat, with his rod over the left side; Cornelia in the stern, with her rod over the right side. The night was cloudy and very black. Each of them had put on the largest possible fly, one a "Bee-Pond" and the other a "Dragon;" but even these were invisible. They measured out the right length of line, and let the flies drift back until they hung over the shoal, in the curly water where the two currents meet.

There were three other boats to the left of them. McTurk was their only neighbour in the darkness on the right. Once they heard

121

him swearing softly to himself, and knew that he had hooked and lost a fish.

Away down at the tail of the pool, dimly visible through the gloom, the furtive fisherman, Parsons, had anchored his boat. No noise ever came from that craft. If he wished to change his position, he did not pull up the anchor and let it down again with a bump. He simply lengthened or shortened his anchor rope. There was no click of the reel when he played a fish. He drew in and paid out the line through the rings by hand, without a sound. What he thought when a fish got away, no one knew, for he never said it. He concealed his angling as if it had been a conspiracy. Twice that night they heard a faint splash in the water near his boat, and twice they saw him put his arm over the side in the darkness and bring it back again very quietly.

"That's the second fish for Parsons," whispered Beekman, "what a secretive old Fortunatus he is! He knows more about fishing than any man on the pool, and talks less."

Cornelia did not answer. Her thoughts were all on the tip of her own rod. About eleven o'clock a fine, drizzling rain set in. The fishing was very slack. All the other boats gave it up in despair; but Cornelia said she wanted to stay out a little longer, they might as well finish up the week.

At precisely fifty minutes past eleven, Beekman reeled up his line, and remarked with firmness that the holy Sabbath day was almost at hand and they ought to go in.

"Not till I 've landed this trout," said Cornelia.

"What? A trout! Have you got one?"

"Certainly; I 've had him on for at least fifteen minutes. I 'm playing him Mr. Parsons' way. You might as well light the lantern and get the net ready; he 's coming in towards the boat now."

Beekman broke three matches before he made the lantern burn; and when he held it up over the gunwale, there was the trout sure enough, gleaming ghostly pale in the dark water, close to the boat, and quite tired out. He slipped the net over the fish and drew it in,—a monster.

"I 'll carry that trout, if you please," said Cornelia, as they stepped out of the boat; and she walked into the camp, on the last stroke of midnight, with the fish in her hand, and quietly asked for the steelyard.

Eight pounds and fourteen ounces,—that was the weight. Everybody was amazed. It was the "best fish" of the year. Cornelia showed no sign of exultation, until just as John was carrying the trout to the ice-house. Then she flashed out:—

"Quite a fair imitation, Mr. McTurk,—isn't it?"

Now McTurk's best record for the last fifteen years was seven pounds and twelve ounces.

So far as McTurk is concerned, this is the end of the story. But not for the De Peysters. I wish it were. Beekman went to sleep that night with a contented spirit. He felt that his experiment in education had been a success. He had made his wife an angler.

He had indeed, and to an extent which he little suspected. That Upper Dam trout was to her like the first taste of blood to the tiger. It seemed to change, at once, not so much her character as the direction of her vital energy. She yielded to the lunacy of angling, not by slow degrees, (as first a transient delusion, then a fixed idea, then a chronic infirmity, finally a mild insanity,) but by a sudden plunge into the most violent mania. So far from being ready to die at Upper Dam, her desire now was to live there—and to live solely for the sake of fishing—as long as the season was open.

There were two hundred and forty hours left to midnight on the thirtieth of September. At least two hundred of these she spent on the pool; and when Beekman was too exhausted to manage the boat and the net and the lantern for her, she engaged a trustworthy guide to take Beekman's place while he slept. At the end of the last day her score was twenty-three, with an average of five pounds and a quarter. His score was nine, with an average of four pounds. He had succeeded far beyond his wildest hopes.

The next year his success became even more astonishing. They went to the Titan Club in Canada. The ugliest and most inaccessible sheet of water in that territory is Lake Pharaoh. But it is famous for the extraordinary fishing at a certain spot near the outlet, where there is just room enough for one canoe. They camped on Lake Pharaoh for six weeks, by Mrs. De Peyster's command; and her canoe was always the first to reach the fishing-ground in the morning, and the last to leave it in the evening.

Some one asked him, when he returned to the city, whether he had good luck.

"Quite fair," he tossed off in a careless way; "we took over three hundred pounds."

"To your own rod?" asked the inquirer, in admiration.

"No-o-o," said Beekman, "there were two of us."

125

There were two of them, also, the following year, when they joined the Natasheebo Salmon Club and fished that celebrated river in Labrador. The custom of drawing lots every night for the water that each member was to angle over the next day, seemed to be especially designed to fit the situation. Mrs. De Peyster could fish her own pool and her husband's too. The result of that year's fishing was something phenomenal. She had a score that made a paragraph in the newspapers and called out editorial comment. One editor was so inadequate to the situation as to entitle the article in which he described her triumph "The Equivalence of Woman." It was well-meant, but she was not at all pleased with it.

She was now not merely an angler, but a "record" angler of the most virulent type. Wherever they went, she wanted, and she got, the pick of the water. She seemed to be equally at home on all kinds of streams, large and small. She would pursue the little mountain-brook trout in the early spring, and the Labrador salmon in July, and the huge speckled trout of the northern lakes in September, with the same avidity and resolution. All that she cared for was to get the best and the most of the fishing at each place where she angled. This she always did.

A FATAL SUCCESS

And Beekman,—well, for him there were no more long separations from the partner of his life while he went off to fish some favourite stream. There were no more home-comings after a good day's sport to find her clad in cool and dainty raiment on the verandah, ready to welcome him with friendly badinage. There was not even any casting of the fly around Hardscrabble Point while she sat in the canoe reading a novel, looking up with mild and pleasant interest when he caught a larger fish than usual, as an older and wiser person looks at a child playing some innocent game. Those days of a divided interest between man and wife were gone. She was now fully converted, and more. Beekman and Cornelia were one; and she was the one.

The last time I saw the De Peysters he was following her along the Beaverkill, carrying a landing-net and a basket, but no rod. She paused for a moment to exchange greetings, and then strode on down the stream. He lingered for a few minutes longer to light a pipe.

"Well, old man," I said, "you certainly have succeeded in making an angler of Mrs. De Peyster."

"Yes, indeed," he answered,—"have n't I?" Then he continued, after a few thoughtful puffs of smoke, "Do you know, I'm not quite so sure as I used to be that fishing is the best of all sports. I sometimes think of giving it up and going in for croquet."

FISHING IN BOOKS

"SIMPSON.—*Have you ever seen any American books on angling, Fisher?*"
"FISHER.—*No. I do not think there are any published. Brother Jonathan is not yet sufficiently civilized to produce anything original on the gentle art. There is good trout-fishing in America, and the streams, which are all free, are much less fished than in our Island, 'from the small number of gentlemen,' as an American writer says, 'who are at leisure to give their time to it.'*"—WILLIAM ANDREW CHATTO: *The Angler's Souvenir* (London, 1835).

FISHING IN BOOKS

THAT wise man and accomplished scholar, Sir Henry Wotton, the friend of Izaak Walton and ambassador of King James I. to the republic of Venice, was accustomed to say that "he would rather live five May months than forty Decembers." The reason for this preference was no secret to those who knew him. It had nothing to do with British or Venetian politics. It was simply because December, with all its domestic joys, is practically a dead month in the angler's calendar.

His occupation is gone. The better sort of fish are out of season. The trout are lean and haggard: it is no trick to catch them and no treat to eat them. The salmon, all except the silly kelts, have run out to sea, and the place of their habitation no man knoweth. There is nothing for the angler to do but wait for the return of spring, and meanwhile encourage and sustain his patience with such small consolations in kind as a friendly Providence may put within his reach.

Some solace may be found, on a day of crisp, wintry weather, in the childish diversion of

131

catching pickerel through the ice. This method of taking fish is practised on a large scale and with elaborate machinery by men who supply the market. I speak not of their commercial enterprise and its gross equipage, but of ice-fishing in its more sportive and desultory form, as it is pursued by country boys and the incorrigible village idler.

You choose for this pastime a pond where the ice is not too thick, lest the labour of cutting through should be discouraging; nor too thin, lest the chance of breaking in should be embarrassing. You then chop out, with almost any kind of a hatchet or pick, a number of holes in the ice, making each one six or eight inches in diameter, and placing them about a dozen feet apart. If you happen to know the course of a current flowing through the pond, or the location of a shoal frequented by minnows, you will do well to keep near it. Over each hole you set a small contrivance called a "tilt-up." It consists of two sticks fastened in the middle, at right angles to each other. The stronger of the two is laid across the opening in the ice. The other is thus balanced above the aperture, with a baited hook and line attached to one end, while the other end is adorned with a little flag. For choice, I would have the flags red.

They look gayer, and I imagine they are more lucky.

When you have thus baited and set your tilt-ups,—twenty or thirty of them,—you may put on your skates and amuse yourself by gliding to and fro on the smooth surface of the ice, cutting figures of eight and grapevines and diamond twists, while you wait for the pickerel to begin their part of the performance. They will let you know when they are ready.

A fish, swimming around in the dim depths under the ice, sees one of your baits, fancies it, and takes it in. The moment he tries to run away with it he tilts the little red flag into the air and waves it backward and forward. "Be quick!" he signals all unconsciously; "here I am; come and pull me up!"

When two or three flags are fluttering at the same moment, far apart on the pond, you must skate with speed and haul in your lines promptly.

How hard it is, sometimes, to decide which one you will take first! That flag in the middle of the pond has been waving for at least a minute, but the other, in the corner of the bay, is tilting up and down more violently: it must be a larger fish. Great Dagon! there's another red signal flying, away over by the point! You hesitate, you make a few strokes in one direc-

tion, then you whirl around and dart the other
way. Meantime one of the tilt-ups, constructed
with too short a cross-stick, has been pulled to
one side, and disappears in the hole. One pickerel in the pond carries a flag. Another tilt-up
ceases to move and falls flat upon the ice. The
bait has been stolen. You dash desperately
toward the third flag and pull in the only fish
that is left,—probably the smallest of them all!

A surplus of opportunities does not insure the
best luck.

A room with seven doors—like the famous
apartment in Washington's headquarters at
Newburgh—is an invitation to bewilderment.
I would rather see one fair opening in life than
be confused by three dazzling chances.

There was a good story about fishing through
the ice which formed part of the stock-in-con-
versation of that ingenious woodsman, Martin
Moody, Esquire, of Big Tupper Lake. "'T was
a blame cold day," he said, "and the lines friz
up stiffer 'n a fence-wire, jus' as fast as I pulled
'em in, and my fingers got so dum' frosted I
could n't bait the hooks. But the fish was
thicker and hungrier 'n flies in June. So I jus'
took a piece of bait and held it over one o' the
holes. Every time a fish jumped up to git it,
I 'd kick him out on the ice. I tell ye, sir, I

kicked out more 'n four hundred pounds of
pick'rel that morning. Yaas, 't was a big lot,
I 'low, but then 't was a cold day! I jus'
stacked 'em up solid, like cordwood."

Let us now leave this frigid subject! Iced
fishing is but a chilling and unsatisfactory imitation of real sport. The angler will soon turn
from it with satiety, and seek a better consolation for the winter of his discontent in the entertainment of fishing in books.

Angling is the only sport that boasts the
honour of having given a classic to literature.

Izaak Walton's success with *The Compleat
Angler* was a fine illustration of fisherman's
luck. He set out, with some aid from an adept
in fly-fishing and cookery, named Thomas
Barker, to produce a little "discourse of fish
and fishing" which should serve as a useful
manual for quiet persons inclined to follow the
contemplative man's recreation. He came home
with a book which has made his name beloved
by ten generations of gentle readers, and given
him a secure place in the Pantheon of letters,—
not a haughty eminence, but a modest niche,
all his own, and ever adorned with grateful
offerings of fresh flowers.

This was great luck. But it was well-deserved, and therefore it has not been grudged or envied.

Walton was a man so peaceful and contented, so friendly in his disposition, and so innocent in all his goings, that only three other writers, so far as I know, have ever spoken ill of him.

One was that sour-complexioned Cromwellian trooper, Richard Franck, who wrote in 1658 an envious book entitled *Northern Memoirs, calculated for the Meridian of Scotland, &c., to which is added The Contemplative and Practical Angler.* In this book the furious Franck first pays Walton the flattery of imitation, and then further adorns him with abuse, calling *The Compleat Angler* "an indigested octavo, stuffed with morals from Dubravius and others," and more than hinting that the father of anglers knew little or nothing of "his uncultivated art." Walton was a Churchman and a Loyalist, you see, while Franck was a Commonwealth man and an Independent.

The second detractor of Walton was Lord Byron, who wrote

"*The quaint, old, cruel coxcomb in his gullet
Should have a hook, and a small trout to pull it.*"

But Byron is certainly a poor authority on the quality of mercy. His contempt need not cause an honest man overwhelming distress. I should call it a complimentary dislike.

The third author who expressed unpleasant sentiments in regard to Walton was Leigh Hunt. Here, again, I fancy that partizan prejudice had something to do with the dislike. Hunt was a radical in politics and religion. Moreover there was a feline strain in his character, which made it necessary for him to scratch somebody now and then, as a relief to his feelings.

Walton was a great quoter. His book is not "stuffed," as Franck jealously alleged, but it is certainly well sauced with piquant references to other writers, as early as the author of the Book of Job, and as late as John Dennys, who betrayed to the world *The Secrets of Angling* in 1613. Walton further seasoned his book with fragments of information about fish and fishing, more or less apocryphal, gathered from Ælian, Pliny, Plutarch, Sir Francis Bacon, Dubravius, Gesner, Rondeletius, the learned Aldrovandus, the venerable Bede, the divine Du Bartas, and many others. He borrowed freely for the adornment of his discourse, and did not scorn to make use of what may be called *live quotations*,—that is to say, the unpublished remarks of his near contemporaries, caught in friendly conversation, or handed down by oral tradition.

But these various seasonings did not disguise, they only enhanced, the delicate flavour of the dish which he served up to his readers. This was all of his own taking, and of a sweetness quite incomparable.

I like a writer who is original enough to water his garden with quotations, without fear of being drowned out. Such men are Charles Lamb and James Russell Lowell and John Burroughs.

Walton's book is as fresh as a handful of wild violets and sweet lavender. It breathes the odours of the green fields and the woods. It tastes of simple, homely, appetizing things like the "syllabub of new verjuice in a new-made haycock" which the milkwoman promised to give Piscator the next time he came that way. Its music plays the tune of *A Contented Heart* over and over again without dulness, and charms us into harmony with

> "*A noise like the sound of a hidden brook*
> *In the leafy month of June,*
> *That to the sleeping woods all night*
> *Singeth a quiet tune.*"

Walton has been quoted even more than any of the writers whom he quotes. It would be difficult, even if it were not ungrateful, to write about angling without referring to him. Some pretty saying, some wise reflection from his pages, suggests itself at almost every turn of the subject.

And yet his book, though it be the best, is not the only readable one that his favourite recreation has begotten. The literature of angling is extensive, as any one may see who will look at the list of the collection presented by Mr. John Bartlett to Harvard University, or study the catalogue of the piscatorial library of Mr. Dean Sage, of Albany, who himself has contributed an admirable book on *The Ristigouche*.

Nor is this literature altogether composed of dry and technical treatises, interesting only to the confirmed anglimaniac, or to the young novice ardent in pursuit of practical information. There is a good deal of juicy reading in it.

Books about angling should be divided (according to De Quincey's method) into two classes,—the literature of knowledge, and the literature of power.

The first class contains the handbooks on rods and tackle, the directions how to angle for different kinds of fish, and the guides to various fishing-resorts. The weakness of these books is that they soon fall out of date, as the

139

manufacture of tackle is improved, the art of angling refined, and the fish in once-famous waters are educated or exterminated.

Alas, how transient is the fashion of this world, even in angling! The old manuals with their precise instruction for trimming and painting trout-rods eighteen feet long, and their painful description of "oyntments" made of nettle-juice, fish-hawk oil, camphor, cat's fat, or assafœdita, (supposed to allure the fish,) are altogether behind the age. Many of the flies described by Charles Cotton and Thomas Barker seem to have gone out of style among the trout. Perhaps familiarity has bred contempt. Generation after generation of fish have seen these same old feathered confections floating on the water, and learned by sharp experience that they do not taste good. The *blasé* trout demand something new, something modern. It is for this reason, I suppose, that an altogether original fly, unheard of, startling, will often do great execution in an over-fished pool.

Certain it is that the art of angling, in settled regions, is growing more dainty and difficult. You must cast a longer, lighter line; you must use finer leaders; you must have your flies dressed on smaller hooks.

FISHING IN BOOKS

And another thing is certain: in many places (described in the ancient volumes) where fish were once abundant, they are now like the shipwrecked sailors in Vergil his Æneid,—

"rari nantes in gurgite vasto."

The floods themselves are also disappearing. Mr. Edmund Clarence Stedman was telling me, the other day, of the trout-brook that used to run through the Connecticut village when he nourished a poet's youth. He went back to visit the stream a few years since, and it was gone, literally vanished from the face of earth, stolen to make a water-supply for the town, and used for such base purposes as the washing of clothes and the sprinkling of streets.

I remember an expedition with my father, some twenty years ago, to Nova Scotia, whither we set out to realize the hopes kindled by an *Angler's Guide* written in the early sixties. It was like looking for tall clocks in the farmhouses around Boston. The harvest had been well gleaned before our arrival, and in the very place where our visionary author located his most famous catch we found a summer hotel and a sawmill.

'T is strange and sad, how many regions

there are where "the fishing was wonderful forty years ago"!

The second class of angling books—the literature of power—includes all (even those written with some purpose of instruction) in which the gentle fascinations of the sport, the attractions of living out-of-doors, the beauties of stream and woodland, the recollections of happy adventure, and the cheerful thoughts that make the best of a day's luck, come clearly before the author's mind and find some fit expression in his words. Of such books, thank Heaven, there is a plenty to bring a Maytide charm and cheer into the fisherman's dull December. I will name, by way of random tribute from a grateful but unmethodical memory, a few of these consolatory volumes.

First of all comes a family of books that were born in Scotland and smell of the heather.

Whatever a Scotchman's conscience permits him to do, is likely to be done with vigour and a fiery mind. In trade and in theology, in fishing and in fighting, he is all there and thoroughly kindled.

There is an old-fashioned book called *The Moor and the Loch*, by John Colquhoun, which is full of contagious enthusiasm. Thomas Tod

142

FISHING IN BOOKS

Stoddart was a most impassioned angler, (though over-given to strong language,) and in his *Angling Reminiscences* he has touched the subject with a happy hand,—happiest when he breaks into poetry and tosses out a song for the fisherman. Professor John Wilson of the University of Edinburgh held the chair of Moral Philosophy in that instiution, but his true fame rests on his well-earned titles of M. A. and F. R. S.,—Master of Angling, and Fisherman Royal of Scotland. His *Recreations of Christopher North*, albeit their humour is sometimes too boisterously hammered in, are genial and generous essays, overflowing with passages of good-fellowship and pedestrian fancy. I would recommend any person in a dry and melancholy state of mind to read his paper on "Streams," in the first volume of *Essays Critical and Imaginative*. But it must be said, by way of warning to those with whom dryness is a matter of principle, that all Scotch fishing-books are likely to be sprinkled with Highland Dew.

Among English anglers, Sir Humphry Davy is one of whom Christopher North speaks rather slightingly. Nevertheless his *Salmonia* is well worth reading, not only because it was written by a learned man, but because it exhales the spirit of cheerful piety and vital wisdom. Charles Kingsley was another great man who wrote well about angling. His *Chalk-Stream Studies* are clear and sparkling. They cleanse the mind and refresh the heart and put us more in love with living. Of quite a different style are the *Maxims and Hints for an Angler, and Miseries of Fishing*, which were written by Richard Penn, a grandson of the founder of Pennsylvania. This is a curious and rare little volume, professing to be a compilation from the *Common Place Book of the Houghton Fishing Club*, and dealing with the subject from a Pickwickian point of view. I suppose that William Penn would have thought his grandson a frivolous writer.

But he could not have entertained such an opinion of the Honourable Robert Boyle, of whose *Occasional Reflections* no less than twelve discourses treat "of Angling Improved to Spiritual Uses." The titles of some of these discourses are quaint enough to quote. "Upon the being called upon to rise early on a very fair morning." "Upon the mounting, singing, and lighting of larks." "Upon fishing with a counterfeit fly." "Upon a danger arising from an unseasonable contest with the steersman." "Upon one's drinking water out of the brim of his hat." With such good texts it is easy to endure, and easier still to spare, the sermons.

Englishman carry their love of travel into their anglimania, and many of their books describe fishing adventures in foreign parts. *Rambles with a Fishing-Rod*, by E. S. Roscoe, tells of happy days in the Salzkammergut and the Bavarian Highlands and Normandy. *Fish-Tails and a Few Others*, by Bradnock Hall, contains some delightful chapters on Norway. *The Rod in India*, by H. S. Thomas, narrates wonderful adventures with the Mahseer and the Rohu and other pagan fish.

But, after all, I like the English angler best when he travels at home, and writes of dry-fly fishing in the Itchen or the Test, or of wet-fly fishing in Northumberland or Sutherland-shire. There is a fascinating booklet that appeared quietly, some years ago, called *An Amateur Angler's Days in Dove Dale*. It runs as easily and merrily and kindly as a little river, full of peace and pure enjoyment. Other books of the same quality have since been written by the same pen,—*Days in Clover, Fresh Woods, By Meadow and Stream*. It is no secret, I believe, that the author is Mr. Edward Marston, the senior member of a London publishing-house. But he still clings to his retiring pen-name of "The Amateur Angler," and represents himself, by a graceful fiction, as all unskilled in the art. An instance of similar modesty is found in Mr. Andrew Lang, who entitles the first chapter of his delightful *Angling Sketches* (without which no fisherman's library is complete), "Confessions of a Duffer." This an engaging liberty which no one else would dare to take.

The best English fish-story pure and simple, that I know, is *Crocker's Hole*, by R. D. Blackmore, the creator of *Lorna Doone*.

Let us turn now to American books about angling. Of these the merciful dispensations of Providence have brought forth no small store since Mr. William Andrew Chatto made the ill-natured remark which is pilloried at the head of this chapter. By the way, it seems that Mr. Chatto had never heard of "The Schuylkill Fishing Company," which was founded on that romantic stream near Philadelphia in 1732, nor seen the *Authentic Historical Memoir* of that celebrated and amusing society.

I am sorry for the man who cannot find pleasure in reading the appendix of *The American Angler's Book*, by Thaddeus Norris; or the discursive pages of Frank Forester's *Fish and Fishing;* or the introduction and notes of that unexcelled edition of Walton which was made by the Reverend Doctor George W. Bethune; or *Superior Fishing* and *Game Fish of the North*, by Mr. Robert B. Roosevelt; or Henshall's *Book of the Black Bass;* or the admirable digressions of Mr. Henry P. Wells, in his *Fly-Rods and Fly-Tackle*, and *The American Salmon Angler*. Dr. William C. Prime has never put his profound knowledge of the art of angling into a manual of technical instruction; but he has written of the delights of the sport in *Owl Creek Letters*, and in *I Go A-Fishing*, and in some of the chapters of *Along New England Roads* and *Among New England Hills*, with a persuasive skill that has created many new anglers, and made many old ones grateful. It is a fitting coincidence of heredity that his niece, Mrs. Annie Trumbull Slosson, is the author of the most tender and pathetic of all angling stories, *Fishin' Jimmy*.

But it is not only in books written altogether from his peculiar point of view and to humour his harmless insanity, that the angler may find pleasant reading about his favourite pastime. There are excellent bits of fishing scattered all through the field of good literature. It seems as if almost all the men who could write well

147

had a friendly feeling for the contemplative sport.

Plutarch, in *The Lives of the Noble Grecians and Romans*, tells a capital fish-story of the manner in which the Egyptian Cleopatra fooled that far-famed Roman wight, Marc Antony, when they were angling together on the Nile. As I recall it, from a perusal in early boyhood, Antony was having very bad luck indeed; in fact he had taken nothing, and was sadly put out about it. Cleopatra, thinking to get a rise out of him, secretly told one of her attendants to dive over the opposite side of the barge and fasten a salt fish to the Roman general's hook. The attendant was much pleased with this commission, and, having executed it, proceeded to add a fine stroke of his own; for when he had made the fish fast on the hook, he gave a great pull to the line and held on tightly. Antony was much excited and began to haul violently at his tackle.

"By Jupiter!" he exclaimed, "it was long in coming, but I have a colossal bite now."

"Have a care," said Cleopatra, laughing behind her sunshade, "or he will drag you into the water. You must give him line when he pulls hard."

"Not a denarius will I give!" rudely re-

sponded Antony. "I mean to have this hali-
but or Hades!"

At this moment the man under the boat,
being out of breath, let the line go, and Antony,
falling backward, drew up the salted herring.

"Take that fish off the hook, Palinurus," he
proudly said. "It is not as large as I thought,
but it looks like the oldest one that has been
caught to-day."

Such, in its general effect, is the tale narrated
by the veracious Plutarch. And if any careful
critic wishes to verify my quotation from
memory, he may compare it with the proper
page of Langhorne's translation; I think it is in
the second volume, near the end.

Sir Walter Scott, who once described himself
as

> "*No fisher,*
> *But a well-wisher*
> *To the game,*"

has an amusing passage of angling in the third
chapter of *Redgauntlet*. Darsie Latimer is re-
lating his adventures in Dumfriesshire. "By
the way," says he, "old Cotton's instructions, by
which I hoped to qualify myself for the gentle
society of anglers, are not worth a farthing for
this meridian. I learned this by mere accident,

after I had waited four mortal hours. I shall never forget an impudent urchin, a cowherd, about twelve years old, without either brogue or bonnet, barelegged, with a very indifferent pair of breeches,—how the villain grinned in scorn at my landing-net, my plummet, and the gorgeous jury of flies which I had assembled to destroy all the fish in the river. I was induced at last to lend the rod to the sneering scoundrel, to see what he would make of it; and he not only half-filled my basket in an hour, but literally taught me to kill two trouts with my own hand."

Thus ancient and well-authenticated is the superstition of the angling powers of the barefooted country-boy,—in fiction.

Sir Edward Bulwer Lytton, in that valuable but over-capitalized book, *My Novel*, makes use of Fishing for Allegorical Purposes. The episode of John Burley and the One-eyed Perch not only points a Moral but adorns the Tale.

In the works of R. D. Blackmore, angling plays a less instructive but a pleasanter part. It is closely interwoven with love. There is a magical description of trout-fishing on a meadow-brook in *Alice Lorraine*. And who that has read *Lorna Doone*, (pity for the man or woman that knows not the delight of that book!) can ever forget how young John Ridd dared his way up the gliddery water-slide, after loaches, and found Lorna in a fair green meadow adorned with flowers, at the top of the brook?

I made a little journey into the Doone Country once, just to see that brook and to fish in it. The stream looked smaller, and the water-slide less terrible, than they seemed in the book. But it was a mighty pretty place after all; and I suppose that even John Ridd, when he came back to it in after years, found it shrunken a little.

All the streams were larger in our boyhood than they are now, except, perhaps, that which flows from the sweetest spring of all, the fountain of love, which John Ridd discovered beside the Bagworthy River,—and I, on the willow-shaded banks of the Patapsco, where the Baltimore girls used to fish for gudgeons,—and you? Come, gentle reader, is there no stream whose name is musical to you, because of a hidden spring of love that you once found on its shore? The waters of that fountain never fail, and in them alone we taste the undiminished fulness of immortal youth.

The stories of William Black are enlivened with fish, and he knew, better than most men, how they should be taken. Whenever he wanted to get two young people engaged to each other, all other devices failing, he sent them out to angle together. If it had not been for fishing, everything in *A Princess of Thule* and *White Heather* would have gone wrong.

But even men who have been disappointed in love may angle for solace or diversion. I have known some old bachelors who fished excellently well; and others I have known who could find, and give, much pleasure in a day on the stream, though they had no skill in the sport. Of this class was Washington Irving, with an extract from whose *Sketch Book* I will bring this rambling dissertation to an end.

"Our first essay," says he, "was along a mountain brook among the highlands of the Hudson; a most unfortunate place for the execution of those piscatory tactics which had been invented along the velvet margins of quiet English rivulets. It was one of those wild streams that lavish, among our romantic solitudes, unheeded beauties enough to fill the sketch-book of a hunter of the picturesque. Sometimes it would leap down rocky shelves, making small cascades over which the trees threw their broad balancing sprays, and long nameless weeds hung in fringes from the impending banks, dripping with dia-

152

mond drops. Sometimes it would brawl and
fret along a ravine in the matted shade of a
forest, filling it with murmurs; and, after this
termagant career, would steal forth into open
day, with the most placid, demure face imaginable; as I have seen some pestilent shrew of a
housewife, after filling her home with uproar
and ill-humour, come dimpling out of doors,
swimming and courtesying, and smiling upon
all the world.

"How smoothly would this vagrant brook
glide, at such times, through some bosom of
green meadow-land among the mountains, where
the quiet was only interrupted by the occasional
tinkling of a bell from the lazy cattle among the
clover, or the sound of a woodcutter's axe from
the neighbouring forest!

"For my part, I was always a bungler at all
kinds of sport that required either patience or
adroitness, and had not angled above half an
hour before I had completely 'satisfied the sentiment,' and convinced myself of the truth of
Izaak Walton's opinion, that angling is something like poetry,—a man must be born to it.
I hooked myself instead of the fish; tangled my
line in every tree; lost my bait; broke my rod;
until I gave up the attempt in despair, and

passed the day under the trees, reading old Izaak, satisfied that it was his fascinating vein of honest simplicity and rural feeling that had bewitched me, and not the passion for angling."

A NORWEGIAN HONEYMOON

"*The best rose-bush, after all, is not that which has the fewest thorns, but that which bears the finest roses.*"—SOLOMON SINGLEWITZ: *The Life of Adam.*

A NORWEGIAN HONEYMOON

I

IT was not all unadulterated sweetness, of course. There were enough difficulties in the way to make it seem desirable; and a few stings of annoyance, now and then, lent piquancy to the adventure. But a good memory, in dealing with the past, has the art of straining out all the beeswax of discomfort, and storing up little jars of pure hydromel. As we look back at our six weeks in Norway, we agree that no period of our partnership in experimental honeymooning has yielded more honey to the same amount of comb.

Several considerations led us to the resolve of taking our honeymoon experimentally rather than chronologically. We started from the self-evident proposition that it ought to be the happiest time in married life.

"It is perfectly ridiculous," said my lady Graygown, "to suppose that a thing like that can be fixed by the calendar. It may possibly fall in the first month after the wedding, but it is not likely. Just think how slightly two

157

people know each other when they get married. They are in love, of course, but that is not at all the same as being well acquainted. Sometimes the more love, the less acquaintance! And sometimes the more acquaintance, the less love! Besides, at first there are always the notes of thanks for the wedding-presents to be written, and the letters of congratulation to be answered, and it is awfully hard to make each one sound a little different from the others and perfectly natural. Then, you know, everybody seems to suspect you of the folly of being newly married. You run across your friends everywhere, and they grin when they see you. You can't help feeling as if a lot of people were watching you through opera-glasses, or taking snap-shots at you with a kodak. It is absurd to imagine that the first month must be the real honeymoon. And just suppose it were,—what bad luck that would be! What would there be to look forward to?"

Every word that fell from her lips seemed to me like the wisdom of Diotima.

"You are right," I cried; "Portia could not hold a candle to you for clear argument. Besides, suppose two people are imprudent enough to get married in the first week of December, as we did!—what becomes of the chronological

honeymoon then? There is no fishing in December, and all the rivers of Paradise, at least
in our latitude, are frozen up. No, my lady,
we will discover our month of honey by the
empirical method. Each year we will set out
together to seek it in a solitude for two; and we
will compare notes on moons, and strike the
final balance when we are sure that our happiest
experiment has been completed."

We are not sure of that, even yet. We are
still engaged, as a committee of two, in our
philosophical investigation, and we decline to
make anything but a report of progress. We
know more now than we did when we first went
honeymooning in the city of Washington. For
one thing, we are certain that not even the far-
famed rosemary-fields of Narbonne, or the fragrant hillsides of the Corbières, yield a sweeter
harvest to the busy-ness of the bees than the
Norwegian meadows and mountain-slopes
yielded to our idleness in the summer of 1888.

II

The rural landscape of Norway, on the long
easterly slope that leads up to the watershed
among the mountains of the western coast, is
not unlike that of Vermont or New Hampshire.

FISHERMAN'S LUCK

The railway from Christiania to the Randsfjord carried us through a hilly country of scattered farms and villages. Wood played a prominent part in the scenery. There were dark stretches of forest on the hilltops and in the valleys; rivers filled with floating logs; sawmills beside the waterfalls; wooden farmhouses painted white; and rail-fences around the fields. The people seemed sturdy, prosperous, independent. They had the familiar habit of coming down to the station to see the train arrive and depart. We might have fancied ourselves on a journey through the Connecticut valley, if it had not been for the soft sing-song of the Norwegian speech and the uniform politeness of the railway officials.

What a room that was in the inn at Randsfjord where we spent our first night out! Vast, bare, primitive, with eight windows to admit the persistent nocturnal twilight; a sea-like floor of blue-painted boards, unbroken by a single island of carpet; and a castellated stove in one corner: an apartment for giants, with two little beds for dwarfs on opposite shores of the ocean. There was no telephone; so we arranged a system of communication with a fishing-line, to make sure that the sleepy partner should be awake in time for the early boat in the morning.

160

A NORWEGIAN HONEYMOON

The journey up the lake took seven hours, and reminded us of a voyage on Lake George; placid, picturesque, and pervaded by summer boarders. Somewhere on the way we had lunch, and were well fortified to take the road when the steamboat landed us at Odnaes, at the head of the lake, about two o'clock in the afternoon.

There are several methods in which you may drive through Norway. The government maintains posting-stations at the farms along the main travelled highways, where you can hire horses and carriages of various kinds. There are also English tourist agencies which make a business of providing travellers with complete transportation. You may try either of these methods alone, or you may make a judicious mixture.

Thus, by an application of the theory of permutations and combinations, you have your choice among four ways of accomplishing a driving-tour. First, you may engage a carriage and pair, with a driver, from one of the tourist agencies, and roll through your journey in sedentary ease, provided your horses do not go lame or give out. Second, you may rely altogether upon the posting-stations to send you on your journey; and this is a very pleasant, lively way, provided there is not a crowd of travellers on the road before you, who take up all the comfortable conveyances and leave you nothing but a jolting cart or a ramshackle *kariol* of the time of St. Olaf. Third, you may rent an easy-riding vehicle (by choice a well-hung gig) for the entire trip, and change ponies at the stations as you drive along; this is the safest way. The fourth method is to hire your horseflesh at the beginning for the whole journey, and pick up your vehicles from place to place. This method is theoretically possible, but I do not know any one who has tried it.

Our gig was waiting for us at Odnaes. There was a brisk little mouse-coloured pony in the shafts; and it took but a moment to strap our leather portmanteau on the board at the back, perch the postboy on top of it, and set out for our first experience of a Norwegian driving-tour.

The road at first was level and easy; and we bowled along smoothly through the valley of the Etnaelv, among drooping birch-trees and green fields where the larks were singing. At Tom-levolden, ten miles farther on, we reached the first station, a comfortable old farmhouse, with a great array of wooden outbuildings. Here we had a chance to try our luck with the Norwegian language in demanding, "*en hest, saa straxt som muligt.*" This was what the guidebook told us to say when we wanted a horse.

There is great fun in making a random cast on the surface of a strange language. You cannot tell what will come up. It is like an experiment in witchcraft. We should not have been at all surprised, I must confess, if our preliminary incantation had brought forth a cow or a basket of eggs.

But the good people seemed to divine our intentions; and while we were waiting for one of the stable-boys to catch and harness the new horse, a yellow-haired maiden inquired, in very fair English, if we would not be pleased to have a cup of tea and some butter-bread; which we did with great comfort.

The *Skydsgut*, or so-called postboy, for the next stage of the journey, was a full-grown man of considerable weight. As he climbed to his perch on our portmanteau, my lady Graygown congratulated me on the prudence which had provided that one side of that receptacle should be of an inflexible stiffness, quite incapable of being crushed; otherwise, asked she, what would have become of her Sunday frock under the pressure of this stern necessity of a postboy?

But I think we should not have cared very much if all our luggage had been smashed on this journey, for the road now began to ascend, and the views over the Etnadal, with its winding river, were of a breadth and sweetness most consoling. Up and up we went, curving in and out through the forest, crossing wild ravines and shadowy dells, looking back at every turn on the wide landscape bathed in golden light. At the station of Sveen, where we changed horse and postboy again, it was already evening. The sun was down, but the mystical radiance of the northern twilight illumined the sky. The dark fir-woods spread around us, and their odourous breath was diffused through the cool, still air. We were crossing the level summit of the plateau, twenty-three hundred feet above the sea. Two tiny woodland lakes gleamed out among the trees. Then the road began to slope gently towards the west, and emerged suddenly on the edge of the forest, looking out over the long, lovely vale of Valders, with snow-touched mountains on the horizon, and the river Baegna shimmering along its bed, a thousand feet below us.

What a heart-enlarging outlook! What a keen joy of motion, as the wheels rolled down the long incline, and the sure-footed pony swung between the shafts and rattled his hoofs merrily on the hard road! What long, deep breaths of silent pleasure in the crisp night air! What wondrous mingling of lights in the afterglow of sunset, and the primrose bloom of the first stars, and faint foregleamings of the rising moon creeping over the hill behind us! What perfection of companionship without words, as we rode together through a strange land, along the edge of the dark!

When we finished the thirty-fifth mile, and drew up in the courtyard of the station at Frydenlund, Graygown sprang out, with a little sigh of regret.

"Is it last night," she cried, "or to-morrow morning? I have n't the least idea what time it is; it seems as if we had been travelling in eternity."

"It is just ten o'clock," I answered, "and the landlord says there will be a hot supper of trout ready for us in five minutes."

It would be vain to attempt to give a daily record of the whole journey in which we made this fair beginning. It was a most idle and unsystematic pilgrimage. We wandered up and down, and turned aside when fancy beckoned. Sometimes we hurried on as fast as the horses would carry us, driving sixty or seventy miles a day; sometimes we loitered and dawdled, as if we did not care whether we got anywhere or not. If a place pleased us, we stayed and tried the fishing. If we were tired of driving, we took to the water, and travelled by steamer along a fjord, or hired a rowboat to cross from point to point. One day we would be in a good little hotel, with polyglot guests, and serving-maids in stagey Norse costumes,—like the famous inn at Stalheim, which commands the amazing panorama of the Naerodal. Another day we would lodge in a plain farmhouse like the station at Nedre Vasenden, where eggs and fish were the staples of diet, and the farmer's daughter wore the picturesque peasants' dress, with its tall cap, without any dramatic airs. Lakes and rivers, precipices and gorges, waterfalls and glaciers and snowy mountains were our daily repast. We drove over five hundred miles in various kinds of open wagons, *kariols* for one, and *stolkjaerres* for two, after we had left our comfortable gig behind us. We saw the ancient dragon-gabled church of Borgund; and the delightful, showery town of Bergen; and the gloomy cliffs of the Geiranger-Fjord laced with filmy cataracts; and the bewitched crags of the Romsdal; and the wide, desolate landscape of Jerkin; and a hundred other unforgotten scenes. Somehow or other we went, (around and about, and up and down,

166

now on wheels, and now on foot, and now in a boat,) all the way from Christiania to Throndh-jem. My lady Graygown could give you the exact itinerary, for she has been well brought up, and always keeps a diary. All I know is, that we set out from the one city and arrived at the other, and we gathered by the way a collection of instantaneous mental photographs. I am going to turn them over now, and pick out a few of the clearest pictures.

III

Here is the bridge over the Naeselv at Fager-naes. Just below it is a good pool for trout, but the river is broad and deep and swift. It is difficult wading to get out within reach of the fish. I have taken half a dozen small ones and come to the end of my cast. There is a big one lying out in the middle of the river, I am sure. But the water already rises to my hips; another step will bring it over the top of my waders, and send me downstream feet uppermost.

"Take care!" cries Graygown from the grassy bank, where she sits placidly crocheting some mysterious fabric of white yarn.

She does not see the large rock lying at the bottom of the river just beyond me. If I can

step on that, and stand there without being
swept away, I can reach the mid-current with
my flies. It is a long stride and a slippery foot-
hold, but by good luck "the last step which
costs" is accomplished. The tiny black and
orange hackle goes curling out over the stream,
lights softly, and swings around with the current, folding and expanding its feathers as if it
were alive. The big trout takes it promptly
the instant it passes over him; and I play him
and net him without moving from my perilous
perch.

Graygown waves her crochet-work like a
flag, "Bravo!" she cries. "That's a beauty,
nearly two pounds! But do be careful about
coming back; you are not good enough to take
any risks yet."

The station at Skogstad is a solitary farmhouse lying far up on the bare hillside, with its
barns and out-buildings grouped around a central courtyard, like a rude fortress. The river
travels along the valley below, now wrestling
its way through a narrow passage among the
rocks, now spreading out at leisure in a green
meadow. As we cross the bridge, the crystal
water is changed to opal by the sunset glow,
and a gentle breeze ruffles the long pools, and

the trout are rising freely. It is the perfect hour for fishing. Would Graygown dare to drive on alone to the gate of the fortress, and blow upon the long horn which doubtless hangs beside it, and demand admittance and a lodging, "in the name of the great Jehovah and the Continental Congress,"—while I angle down the river a mile or so?

Certainly she would. What door is there in Europe at which the American girl is afraid to knock? "But wait a moment. How do you ask for fried chicken and pancakes in Norwegian? *Kylling og Pandekage?* How fierce it sounds! All right now. Run along and fish."

The river welcomes me like an old friend. The tune that it sings is the same that the flowing water repeats all around the world. Not otherwise do the lively rapids carry the familiar air, and the larger falls drone out a burly bass, along the west branch of the Penobscot, or down the valley of the Bouquet. But here there are no forests to conceal the course of the stream. It lies as free to the view as a child's thought. As I follow on from pool to pool, picking out a good trout here and there, now from a rocky corner edged with foam, now from a swift gravelly run, now from a snug hiding-place that the current has hollowed out beneath

169

the bank, all the way I can see the fortress far above me on the hillside.

I am as sure that it has already surrendered to Graygown as if I could discern her white banner of crochet-work floating from the battlements.

Just before dark, I climb the hill with a heavy basket of fish. The castle gate is open. The scent of chicken and pancakes salutes the weary pilgrim. In a cosy little parlour, adorned with fluffy mats and pictures framed in pine-cones, lit by a hanging lamp with glass pendants, sits the mistress of the occasion, calmly triumphant and plying her crochet-needle.

There is something mysterious about a woman's fancy-work. It seems to have all the soothing charm of the tobacco-plant, without its inconveniences. Just to see her tranquillity, while she relaxes her mind and busies her fingers with a bit of tatting or embroidery or crochet, gives me a sense of being domesticated, a "homey" feeling, anywhere in the wide world.

If you ever go to Norway, you must be sure to see the Loenvand. You can set out from the comfortable hotel at Faleide, go up the Indvik Fjord in a rowboat, cross over a two-mile hill on foot or by carriage, spend a happy day on the

lake, and return to your inn in time for a late
supper. The lake is perhaps the most beautiful
in Norway. Long and narrow, it lies like a priceless emerald, hidden and guarded by jealous
mountains. It is fed by huge glaciers, which
hang over the shoulders of the hills like ragged
cloaks of ice.

As we row along the shore, trolling in vain for
the trout that live in the ice-cold water, fragments of the tattered cloth-of-silver far above
us, on the opposite side, are loosened by the
touch of the summer sun, and fall from the
precipice. They drift downward, at first, as
noiselessly as thistledown; then they strike
the rocks and come crashing towards the lake
with the hollow roar of an avalanche.

At the head of the lake we find ourselves in
an enormous amphitheatre of mountains. Glaciers are peering down upon us. Snow-fields
glare at us with glistening eyes. Black crags
seem to bend above us with an eternal frown.
Streamers of foam float from the forehead of
the hills and the lips of the dark ravines. But
there is a little river of cold, pure water flowing
from one of the rivers of ice, and a pleasant
shelter of young trees and bushes growing
among the débris of shattered rocks; and there
we build our camp-fire and eat our lunch.

171

FISHERMAN'S LUCK

Hunger is a most impudent appetite. It makes a man forget all the proprieties. What place is there so lofty, so awful, that he will not dare to sit down in it and partake of food? Even on the side of Mount Sinai, the elders of Israel spread their out-of-door table, "and did eat and drink."

I see the Tarn of the Elk at this moment, just as it looked in the clear sunlight of that August afternoon, ten years ago. Far down in a hollow of the desolate hills it nestles, four thousand feet above the sea. The moorland trail hangs high above it, and, though it is a mile away, every curve of the treeless shore, every shoal and reef in the light green water is clearly visible. With a powerful field-glass one can almost see the large trout for which the pond is famous.

The shelter-hut on the bank is built of rough gray stones, and the roof is leaky to the light as well as to the weather. But there are two beds in it, one for my guide and one for me; and a practicable fireplace, which is soon filled with a blaze of comfort. There is also a random library of novels, which former fishermen have thoughtfully left behind them. I like strong reading in the wilderness. Give me a story with plenty of danger and wholesome fighting in it,—*The*

A NORWEGIAN HONEYMOON

Three Musketeers, or *Treasure Island,* or *The Afghan's Knife.* Intricate studies of social dilemmas and tales of mild philandering seem bloodless and insipid.

The trout in the Tarn of the Elk are large, undoubtedly, but they are also few in number and shy in disposition. Either some of the peasants have been fishing over them with the deadly "otter," or else they belong to that variety of the trout family known as *Trutta damnosa,*—the species which you can see but cannot take. We watched these aggravating fish playing on the surface at sunset; we saw them dart beneath our boat in the early morning; but not until a driving snowstorm set in, about noon of the second day, did we succeed in persuading any of them to take the fly. Then they rose, for a couple of hours, with amiable perversity. I caught five, weighing between two and four pounds each, and stopped because my hands were so numb that I could cast no longer.

Now for a long tramp over the hills and home. Yes, home; for yonder in the white house at Drivstuen, with fuchsias and geraniums blooming in the windows, and a pretty, friendly Norse girl to keep her company, my lady is waiting for me. See, she comes running out to the door, in the gathering dusk, with a red flower in her hair, and hails me with the fisherman's greeting. *What luck?*

Well, *this* luck, at all events! I can show you a few good fish, and sit down with you to a supper of reindeer-venison and a quiet evening of music and talk.

Shall I forget thee, hospitable Stuefloten, dearest to our memory of all the rustic stations in Norway? There are no stars beside thy name in the pages of Baedeker. But in the book of our hearts a whole constellation is thine. The long, low, white farmhouse stands on a green hill at the head of the Romsdal. A flourishing crop of grass and flowers grows on the stable-roof, and there is a little belfry with a big bell to call the labourers home from the fields. In the corner of the living-room of the old house there is a broad fireplace built across the angle. Curious cupboards are tucked away everywhere. The long table in the dining-room groans thrice a day with generous fare. There are as many kinds of hot bread as in a Virginia country-house; the cream is thick enough to make a spoon stand up in amazement; once, at dinner, we sat embarrassed before six different varieties of pudding.

A NORWEGIAN HONEYMOON

In the evening, when the saffron light is beginning to fade, we go out and walk in the road before the house, looking down the long mystical vale of the Rauma, or up to the purple western hills from which the clear streams of the Ulvaa flow to meet us.

Above Stuefloten the Rauma lingers and meanders through a smoother and more open valley, with broad beds of gravel and flowery meadows. Here the trout and grayling grow fat and lusty, and here we angle for them, day after day, in water so crystalline that when one steps into the stream one hardly knows whether to expect a depth of six inches or six feet.

Tiny English flies and leaders of gossamer are the tackle for such water in midsummer. With this delicate outfit, and with a light hand and a long line, one may easily outfish the native angler, and fill a twelve-pound basket every fair day. I remember an old Norwegian, an inveterate fisherman, whose footmarks we saw ahead of us on the stream all through an afternoon. Footmarks I call them; and so they were, literally, for there were only the prints of a single foot to be seen on the banks of sand, and between them, a series of small, round, deep holes.

"What kind of a bird made those marks, Frederik?" I asked my faithful guide.

"That is old Pedersen," he said, "with his wooden leg. He makes a dot after every step. We shall catch him in a little while."

Sure enough, about six o'clock we saw him standing on a grassy point, hurling his line, with a fat worm on the end of it, far across the stream, and letting it drift down with the current. But the water was too fine for that style of fishing, and the poor old fellow had but a half dozen little fish. My creel was already overflowing, so I emptied out all of the grayling into his bag, and went on up the river to complete my tale of trout before dark.

And when the fishing is over, there is Graygown with the wagon, waiting at the appointed place under the trees, beside the road. The sturdy white pony trots gayly homeward. The pale yellow stars blossom out above the hills again, as they did on that first night when we were driving down into the Valders. Frederik leans over the back of the seat, telling us marvellous tales, in his broken English, of the fishing in a certain lake among the mountains, and of the reindeer-shooting on the fjeld beyond it.

"It is sad that you go to-morrow," says he; "but you come back another year, I think, to

176

fish in that lake, and to shoot those rein-deer."

Yes, Frederik, we are coming back to Norway some day, perhaps,—who can tell? It is one of the hundred places that we are vaguely planning to revisit. For, though we did not see the midnight sun there, we saw the honeymoon most distinctly. And it was bright enough to take pictures by its light.

WHO OWNS THE MOUNTAINS?

"*My heart is fixed firm and stable in the belief that ultimately the sunshine and the summer, the flowers and the azure sky, shall become, as it were, interwoven into man's existence. He shall take from all their beauty and enjoy their glory.*"—RICHARD JEFFERIES: *The Life of the Fields.*

WHO OWNS THE MOUNTAINS?

IT was the little lad that asked the question; and the answer also, as you will see, was mainly his.

We had been keeping Sunday afternoon together in our favourite fashion, following out that pleasant text which tells us to "behold the fowls of the air." There is no injunction of Holy Writ less burdensome in acceptance, or more profitable in obedience, than this easy out-of-doors commandment. For several hours we walked in the way of this precept, through the untangled woods that lie behind the Forest Hills Lodge, where a pair of pigeon-hawks had their nest; and around the brambly shores of the small pond, where Maryland yellow-throats and song-sparrows were settled; and under the lofty hemlocks of the fragment of forest across the road, where rare warblers flitted silently among the tree-tops. The light beneath the evergreens was growing dim as we came out from their shadow into the widespread glow of the sunset, on the edge of a grassy hill, overlooking the long valley of the Gale River, and up-looking to the Franconia Mountains.

It was the benediction hour. The placid air of the day shed a new tranquillity over the consoling landscape. The heart of the earth seemed to taste a repose more perfect than that of common days. A hermit-thrush, far up the vale, sang his vesper hymn; while the swallows, seeking their evening meal, circled above the river-fields without an effort, twittering softly, now and then, as if they must give thanks. Slight and indefinable touches in the scene, perhaps the mere absence of the tiny human figures passing along the road or labouring in the distant meadows, perhaps the blue curls of smoke rising lazily from the farmhouse chimneys, or the family groups sitting under the maple-trees before the door, diffused a sabbath atmosphere over the world.

Then said the lad, lying on the grass beside me, "Father, who owns the mountains?"

I happened to have heard, the day before, of two or three lumber companies that had bought some of the woodland slopes; so I told him their names, adding that there were probably a good many different owners, whose claims taken all together would cover the whole Franconia range of hills.

WHO OWNS THE MOUNTAINS?

"Well," answered the lad, after a moment of silence, "I don't see what difference that makes. Everybody can look at them."

They lay stretched out before us in the level sunlight, the sharp peaks outlined against the sky, the vast ridges of forest sinking smoothly towards the valleys, the deep hollows gathering purple shadows in their bosoms, and the little foothills standing out in rounded promontories of brighter green from the darker mass behind them.

Far to the east, the long comb of Twin Mountain extended itself back into the untrodden wilderness. Mount Garfield lifted a clear-cut pyramid through the translucent air. The huge bulk of Lafayette ascended majestically in front of us, crowned with a rosy diadem of rocks. Eagle Cliff and Bald Mountain stretched their line of scalloped peaks across the entrance to the Notch. Beyond that shadowy vale, the swelling summits of Cannon Mountain rolled away to meet the tumbling waves of Kinsman, dominated by one loftier crested billow that seemed almost ready to curl and break out of green silence into snowy foam. Far down the sleeping Landaff valley the undulating dome of Moosilauke trembled in the distant blue.

They were all ours, from crested cliff to wooded

183

base. The solemn groves of firs and spruces, the plumed sierras of lofty pines, the stately pillared forests of birch and beech, the wild ravines, the tremulous thickets of silvery poplar, the bare peaks with their wide outlooks, and the cool vales resounding with the ceaseless song of little rivers,—we knew and loved them all; they ministered peace and joy to us; they were all ours, though we held no title deeds and our ownership had never been recorded.

What is property, after all? The law says there are two kinds, real and personal. But it seems to me that the only real property is that which is truly personal, that which we take into our inner life and make our own forever, by understanding and admiration and sympathy and love. This is the only kind of possession that is worth anything.

A gallery of great paintings adorns the house of the Honourable Midas Bond, and every year adds a new treasure to his collection. He knows how much they cost him, and he keeps the run of the quotations at the auction sales, congratulating himself as the price of the works of his well-chosen artists rises in the scale, and the value of his art treasures is enhanced. But why should he call them his? He is only their custodian. He keeps them well varnished and

WHO OWNS THE MOUNTAINS?

framed in gilt. But he never passes through those gilded frames into the world of beauty that lies behind the painted canvas. He knows nothing of those lovely places from which the artist's soul and hand have drawn their inspiration. They are closed and barred to him. He has bought the pictures, but he cannot buy the key. The poor art student who wanders through his gallery, lingering with awe and love before the masterpieces, owns them far more truly than Midas does.

Pomposus Silverman purchased a rich library a few years ago. The books were rare and costly. That was the reason why Pomposus bought them. He was proud to feel that he was the possessor of literary treasures which were not to be found in the houses of his wealthiest acquaintances. But the threadbare Bücherfreund, who was engaged at a slender salary to catalogue the library and take care of it, became the real proprietor. Pomposus paid for the books, but Bücherfreund enjoyed them.

I do not mean to say that the possession of much money is always a barrier to real wealth of mind and heart. Nor would I maintain that all the poor of this world are rich in faith and heirs of the kingdom. But some of them are. And if some of the rich of this world (through

185

the grace of Him with whom all things are possible) are also modest in their tastes, and gentle in their hearts, and open in their minds, and ready to be pleased with unbought pleasures, they simply share in the best things which are provided for all.

I speak not now of the strife that men wage over the definition and the laws of property. Doubtless there is much here that needs to be set right. There are men and women in the world who are shut out from the right to earn a living, so poor that they must perish for want of daily bread, so full of misery that there is no room for the tiniest seed of joy in their lives. This is the lingering shame of civilization. Some day, perhaps, we shall find the way to banish it. Some day, every man shall have his title to a share in the world's great work and the world's large joy.

But meantime it is certain that, where there are a hundred poor bodies who suffer from physical privation, there are a thousand poor souls who suffer from spiritual poverty. To relieve this greater suffering there needs no change of laws, only a change of heart.

What does it profit a man to be the landed proprietor of countless acres unless he can reap the harvest of delight that blooms from every rood of God's earth for the seeing eye and the loving spirit? And who can reap that harvest so closely that there shall not be abundant gleaning left for all mankind? The most that a wide estate can yield to its legal owner is a living. But the real owner can gather from a field of goldenrod, shining in the August sunlight, an unearned increment of delight.

We measure success by accumulation. The measure is false. The true measure is appreciation. He who loves most has most.

How foolishly we train ourselves for the work of life! We give our most arduous and eager efforts to the cultivation of those faculties which will serve us in the competitions of the forum and the market-place. But if we were wise, we should care infinitely more for the unfolding of those inward, secret, spiritual powers by which alone we can become the owners of anything that is worth having. Surely God is the great proprietor. Yet all His works He has given away. He holds no title-deeds. The one thing that is His, is the perfect understanding, the perfect joy, the perfect love, of all things that He has made. To a share in this high ownership He welcomes all who are poor in spirit. This is the earth which the meek inherit. This is the patrimony of the saints in light.

FISHERMAN'S LUCK

"Come, laddie," I said to my comrade, "let us go home. You and I are very rich. We own the mountains. But we can never sell them, and we don't want to."

A LAZY, IDLE BROOK

"*Perpetual devotion to what a man calls his business is only to be sustained by perpetual neglect of many other things. And it is not by any means certain that a man's business is the most important thing he has to do.*"—ROBERT LOUIS STEVENSON: *An Apology for Idlers.*

A LAZY, IDLE BROOK

I

ON the South Shore of Long Island, all things incline to a natural somnolence. There are no ambitious mountains, no braggart cliffs, no hasty torrents, no bustling waterfalls in that land,

"In which it seemeth always afternoon."

The salt meadows sleep in the summer sun; the farms and market-gardens yield a placid harvest to a race of singularly unhurried tillers of the soil; the low hills rise with gentle slopes, not caring to get too high in the world, only far enough to catch a pleasant glimpse of the sea and a breath of salt air; the very trees grow leisurely, as if they felt that they had "all the time there is." And from this dreamy land, close as it lies to the unresting ocean, the tumult of the breakers and the foam of ever-turning tides are shut off by the languid lagoons of the Great South Bay and a long range of dunes,

191

crested with wire-grass, bay-bushes, and wild-roses.

In such a country you could not expect a little brook to be noisy, fussy, energetic. If it were not lazy, it would be out of keeping.

But the actual and undisguised idleness of this particular brook was another affair, and one in which it was distinguished among its fellows. For almost all the other little rivers of the South Shore, lazy as they may be by nature, yet manage to do some kind of work before they finish the journey from their crystal-clear springs into the brackish waters of the bay. They turn the wheels of sleepy gristmills, while the miller sits with his hands in his pockets underneath the willow-trees. They fill reservoirs out of which great steam-engines pump the water to quench the thirst of Brooklyn. Even the smaller streams tarry long enough in their seaward sauntering to irrigate a few cranberry-bogs and so provide that savoury sauce which makes the Long Island turkey a fitter subject for Thanksgiving.

But this brook of which I speak did none of these useful things. It was absolutely out of business. There was not a mill, nor a reservoir, nor a cranberry-bog, on all its course of a short mile. The only profitable affair it ever undertook was to fill a small ice-pond near its entrance into the Great South Bay. You could hardly call this a very energetic enterprise. It amounted to little more than a good-natured consent to allow itself to be used by the winter for the making of ice, if the winter happened to be cold enough. Even this passive industry came to nothing; for the water, being separated from the bay only by a short tideway under a wooden bridge on the south country road, was too brackish to freeze easily; and the ice, being pervaded with weeds, was not much relished by the public. So the wooden ice-house, innocent of paint, and toned by the weather to a soft, sad-coloured gray, stood like an improvised ruin among the pine-trees beside the pond.

It was through this unharvested ice-pond, this fallow field of water, that my lady Graygown and I entered on acquaintance with our lazy, idle brook. We had a house, that summer, a few miles down the bay. But it was a very small house, and the room that we like best was out of doors. So we spent much time in a sailboat,—by name "The Patience,"—making voyages of exploration into watery corners and byways. Sailing past the wooden bridge one day, when a strong east wind had made a very low tide, we observed the water flowing out beneath the road with an eddying current. We were interested to discover where such a stream came from. But the sailboat could not go under the bridge, nor even make a landing on the shore without risk of getting aground. The next day we came back in a rowboat to follow the clue of curiosity. The tide was high now, and we passed with the reversed current under the bridge, almost bumping our heads against the timbers. Emerging upon the pond, we rowed across its shallow, weed-encumbered waters, and were introduced without ceremony to one of the most agreeable brooks that we had ever met.

It was quite broad where it came into the pond,—a hundred feet from side to side,—bordered with flags and rushes and feathery meadow grasses. The real channel meandered in sweeping curves from bank to bank, and the water, except in the swifter current, was filled with an amazing quantity of some aquatic moss. The woods came straggling down on either shore. There were fallen trees in the stream here and there. On one of the points an old swamp-maple, with its decrepit branches and its leaves already touched with the hectic colours of decay, hung far out over the water which was undermining it, looking and leaning downward,

194

like an aged man who bends, half-sadly and half-willingly, towards the grave.

But for the most part the brook lay wide open to the sky, and the tide, rising and sinking somewhat irregularly in the pond below, made curious alternations in its depth and in the swiftness of its current. For about half a mile we navigated this lazy little river, and then we found that rowing would carry us no farther, for we came to a place where the stream issued with a livelier flood from an archway in a thicket.

This woodland portal was not more than four feet wide, and the branches of the small trees were closely interwoven overhead. We shipped the oars and took one of them for a paddle. Stooping down, we pushed the boat through the archway and found ourselves in the Fairy Dell. It was a long, narrow bower, perhaps four hundred feet from end to end, with the brook dancing through it in a joyous, musical flow over a bed of clean yellow sand and white pebbles. There were deep places in the curves where you could hardly touch bottom with an oar, and shallow places in the straight runs where the boat would barely float. Not a ray of unbroken sunlight leaked through the green roof of this winding corridor; and all along the sides there were delicate mosses and tall ferns and wildwood flowers that love the shade.

At the upper end of the bower our progress in the boat was barred by a low bridge, on a forgotten road that wound through the pine-woods. Here I left my lady Graygown, seated on the shady corner of the bridge with a book, swinging her feet over the stream, while I set out to explore its further course. Above the wood-road there were no more fairy dells, nor easy-going estuaries. The water came down through the most complicated piece of under-brush that I have ever encountered. Alders and swamp maples and pussy-willows and gray birches grew together in a wild confusion. Blackberry bushes and fox-grapes and cat-briers trailed and twisted themselves in an incredible tangle. There was only one way to advance, and that was to wade in the middle of the brook, stooping low, lifting up the pendulous alder-branches, threading a tortuous course, now under and now over the innumerable ob-stacles, as a darning-needle is pushed in and out through the yarn of a woollen stocking.

It was dark and lonely in that difficult pas-sage. The brook divided into many channels, turning this way and that way, as if it were lost in the woods. There were huge clumps of *Os-*

munda regalis spreading their fronds in tropical profusion. Mouldering logs were covered with moss. The water gurgled slowly into deep corners under the banks. Catbirds and blue jays fluttered screaming from the thickets. Cotton-tailed rabbits darted away, showing the white flag of fear. Once I thought I saw the fuscous gleam of a red fox stealing silently through the brush. It would have been no surprise to hear the bark of a raccoon, or see the eyes of a wildcat gleaming through the leaves.

For more than an hour I was pushing my way through this miniature wilderness of half a mile; and then I emerged suddenly, to find myself face to face with a railroad embankment and the afternoon express, with its parlour-cars, thundering down to Southampton!

It was a strange and startling contrast. The explorer's joy, the sense of adventure, the feeling of wildness and freedom, withered and crumpled somewhat preposterously at the sight of the parlour-cars. My scratched hands and wet boots and torn coat seemed unkempt and disreputable. Perhaps some of the well-dressed people looking out at the windows of the train were the friends with whom we were to dine on Saturday. *Batêche !* What would they say to such a costume as mine? What did I care what they said!

But, all the same, it was a shock, a disenchantment, to find that civilization, with all its absurdities and conventionalities, was so threateningly close to my new-found wilderness. My first enthusiasm was not a little chilled as I walked back, along an open woodland path, to the bridge where Graygown was placidly reading. Reading, I say, though her book was closed, and her brown eyes were wandering over the green leaves of the thicket and the white clouds drifting, drifting lazily across the blue deep of the sky.

II

A BETTER ACQUAINTANCE

On the voyage home, she gently talked me out of my disappointment, and into a wiser frame of mind.

It was a surprise, of course, she admitted, to find that our wilderness was so little, and to discover the trail of a parlour-car on the edge of Paradise. But why not turn the surprise around, and make it pleasant instead of disagreeable? Why not look at the contrast from the side that we liked best?

A LAZY, IDLE BROOK

It was not necessary that everybody should take the same view of life that pleased us. The world would not get on very well without people who preferred parlour-cars to canoes, and patent-leather shoes to India-rubber boots, and ten-course dinners to picnics in the woods. These good people were unconsciously toiling at the hard and necessary work of life in order that we, of the chosen and fortunate few, should be at liberty to enjoy the best things in the world.

Why should we neglect our opportunities, which were also our real duties? The nervous disease of civilization might prevail all around us, but that ought not to destroy our grateful enjoyment of the lucid intervals that were granted to us by a merciful Providence.

Why should we not take this little untamed brook, running its humble course through the borders of civilized life and midway between two flourishing summer resorts,—a brook without a single house or a cultivated field on its banks, as free and beautiful and secluded as if it flowed through miles of trackless forest,—why not take this brook as a sign that the ordering of the universe had a "good intention" even for inveterate idlers, and that the great Arranger of the world felt some kindness for such gipsy-hearts as ours? What law, human or divine,

199

was there to prevent us from making this stream our symbol of deliverance from the conventional and commonplace, our guide to liberty and a quiet mind?

So reasoned Graygown with her

> *"most silver flow'*
> *Of subtle-pacéd counsel in distress."*

And, according to her word, so did we. That lazy, idle brook became to us one of the best of friends; the pathfinder of happiness on many a bright summer day; and, through long vacations, the faithful encourager of indolence.

Indolence in the proper sense of the word, you understand. The meaning which is commonly given to it, as Archbishop Trench pointed out in his suggestive book about *Words and Their Uses*, is altogether false. To speak of indolence as if it were a vice is just a great big verbal slander.

Indolence is a virtue. It comes from two Latin words, which mean freedom from anxiety or grief. And that is a wholesome state of mind. There are times and seasons when it is even a pious and blessed state of mind. Not to be in a hurry; not to be ambitious or jealous or resentful; not to feel envious of anybody; not to fret about to-day nor worry about to-morrow,—that is the way we ought all to feel at some time in our lives; and that is the kind of indolence in which our brook faithfully encouraged us.

'T is an age in which such encouragement is greatly needed. We have fallen so much into the habit of being always busy that we know not how nor when to break it off with firmness. Our business tags after us into the midst of our pleasures, and we are ill at ease beyond reach of the telegraph and the daily newspaper. We agitate ourselves amazingly about a multitude of affairs,—the politics of Europe, the state of the weather all around the globe, the marriages and festivities of very rich people, and the latest novelties in crime, none of which are of vital interest to us. The more earnest souls among us are cultivating a vicious tendency to Summer Schools, and Seaside Institutes of Philosophy, and Mountaintop Seminaries of Modern Languages.

We toil assiduously to cram something more into those scrap-bags of knowledge which we fondly call our minds. Seldom do we rest tranquil long enough to find out whether there is anything in them already that is of real value, —any native feeling, any original thought, which would like to come out and sun itself for a while in quiet.

For my part, I am sure that I stand more in

need of a deeper sense of contentment with life than of a knowledge of the Bulgarian tongue, and that all the paradoxes of Hegel would not do me so much good as one hour of vital sympathy with the careless play of children. The Marquis du Paty de l'Huitre may espouse the daughter and heiress of the Honourable James Bulger with all imaginable pomp, if he will. *Ça ne m'intrigue point du tout.* I would rather stretch myself out on the grass and watch yonder pair of kingbirds carrying luscious flies to their young ones in the nest, or chasing away the marauding crow with shrill cries of anger.

What a pretty battle it is, and in a good cause, too! Waste no pity on that big black ruffian. He is a villain and a thief, an egg-stealer, an ogre, a devourer of unfledged innocents. The kingbirds are not afraid of him, knowing that he is a coward at heart. They fly upon him, now from below, now from above. They buffet him from one side and from the other. They circle round him like a pair of swift gunboats round an antiquated man-of-war. They even perch upon his back and dash their beaks into his neck and pluck feathers from his piratical plumage. At last his lumbering flight has carried him far enough away, and the brave little defenders fly back to the nest, poising above it on quivering wings for a moment, then dipping down swiftly in pursuit of some passing insect. The war is over. Courage has had its turn. Now tenderness comes into play. The young birds, all ignorant of the passing danger, but always conscious of an insatiable hunger, are uttering loud remonstrances and plaintive demands for food. Domestic life begins again, and they that sow not, neither gather into barns, are fed.

Do you suppose that this wondrous stage of earth was set, and all the myriad actors on it taught to play their parts, without a spectator in view? Do you think that there is anything better for you and me to do, now and then, than to sit down quietly in a humble seat, and watch a few scenes in the drama? Has it not something to say to us, and do we not understand it best when we have a peaceful heart and free from dolor? That is what *in-dolence* means, and there are no better teachers of it than the light-hearted birds and untoiling flowers, commended by the wisest of all masters to our consideration; nor can we find a more pleasant pedagogue to lead us to their school than a small, merry brook.

And this was what our chosen stream did for

us. It was always luring us away from an artificial life into restful companionship with nature.

Suppose, for example, we found ourselves growing a bit dissatisfied with the domestic arrangements of our little cottage, and coveting the splendours of a grander establishment. An afternoon on the brook was a good cure for that folly. Or suppose a day came when there was an imminent prospect of many formal calls. We had an important engagement up the brook; and while we kept it we could think with satisfaction of the joy of our callers when they discovered that they could discharge their whole duty with a piece of pasteboard. This was an altruistic pleasure. Or suppose that a few friends were coming to supper, and there were no flowers for the supper-table. We could easily have bought them in the village. But it was far more to our liking to take the children up the brook, and come back with great bunches of wild white honeysuckle and blue flag, or posies of arrow-heads and cardinal-flowers. Or suppose that I was very unwisely and reluctantly labouring at some serious piece of literary work, promised for the next number of *The Scribbler's Review*; and suppose that in the midst of this labour the sad news came to me that the fishman had forgotten to leave any fish at our cottage that morning. Should my innocent babes and my devoted wife be left to perish of starvation while I continued my poetical comparison of the two Williams, Shakspeare and Watson? Inhuman selfishness! Of course it was my plain duty to sacrifice my inclinations, and get my fly-rod, and row away across the bay, with a deceptive appearance of cheerfulness, to catch a basket of trout in——

III

THE SECRETS OF INTIMACY

There ! I came within eight letters of telling the name of the brook, a thing that I am firmly resolved not to do. If it were an ordinary fishless little river, or even a stream with nothing better than grass-pike and sunfish in it, you should have the name and welcome. But when a brook contains speckled trout, and when their presence is known to a very few persons who guard the secret as the dragon guarded the golden apples of the Hesperides, and when the size of the trout is large beyond the dreams of hope,—well, when did you know a true angler who would willingly give away the name of such a brook as that? You may find an encourager of indolence in almost any stream of

205

the South Side, and I wish you joy of your brook. But if you want to catch trout in mine you must discover it for yourself, or perhaps go with me some day, and solemnly swear secrecy.

That was the way in which the freedom of the stream was conferred upon me. There was a small boy in the village, the son of rich but respectable parents, and an inveterate all-round sportsman, aged fourteen years, with whom I had formed a close intimacy. I was telling him about the pleasure of exploring the idle brook, and expressing the opinion that in bygone days, (in that mythical "forty years ago" when all fishing was good), there must have been trout in it. A certain look came over the boy's face. He gazed at me solemnly, as if he were searching the inmost depths of my character before he spoke.

"Say, do you want to know something?"

I assured him that an increase of knowledge was the chief aim of my life.

"Do you promise you won't tell?"

I expressed my readiness to be bound to silence by the most awful pledge that the law would sanction.

"Wish you may die?"

I not only wished that I might die, but was perfectly certain that I would die.

A LAZY, IDLE BROOK

"Well, what's the matter with catching trout in that brook now? Do you want to go with me next Saturday? I saw four or five bully ones last week, and got three."

On the appointed day we made the voyage, landed at the upper bridge, walked around by the woodpath to the railroad embankment, and began to worm our way down through the tangled wilderness. Fly-fishing, of course, was out of the question. The only possible method of angling was to let the line, baited with a juicy "garden hackle," drift down the current as far as possible before you, under the alder-branches and the cat-briers, into the holes and corners of the stream. Then, if there came a gentle tug on the rod, you must strike, to one side or the other, as the branches might allow, and trust wholly to luck for a chance to play the fish. Many a trout we lost that day,—the largest ones, of course,—and many a hook was embedded in a sunken log, or hopelessly entwined among the boughs overhead. But when we came out at the bridge, very wet and disheveled, we had seven pretty fish, the heaviest about half a pound. The Fairy Dell yielded a brace of smaller ones, and altogether we were reasonably happy as we took up the oars and pushed out upon the open stream.

But if there were fish above, why should there not be fish below? It was about sunset, the angler's golden hour. We were already committed to the crime of being late for supper. It would add little to our guilt and much to our pleasure to drift slowly down the middle of the brook and cast the artful fly in the deeper corners on either shore. So I took off the vulgar bait-hook and put on a delicate leader with a Queen of the Water for a tail-fly and a Yellow Sally for a dropper,—innocent little confections of feathers and tinsel, dressed on the tiniest hooks, and calculated to tempt the appetite or the curiosity of the most capricious trout.

For a long time the whipping of the water produced no result, and it seemed as if the dainty style of angling were destined to prove less profitable than plain fishing with a worm. But presently we came to an elbow of the brook, just above the estuary, where there was quite a stretch of clear water along the lower side, with two half-sunken logs sticking out from the bank, against which the current had drifted a broad raft of weeds. I made a long cast, and sent the tail-fly close to the edge of the weeds. There was a swelling ripple on the surface of the water, and a noble fish darted from under the logs,

208

dashed at the fly, missed it, and whirled back to his shelter.

"Gee!" said the boy, "that was a whacker! He made a wake like a steamboat."

It was a moment for serious thought. What was best to be done with that fish? Leave him to settle down for the night and come back after him another day? Or try another cast for him at once? A fish on Saturday evening is worth two on Monday morning. I changed the Queen of the Water for a Royal Coachman tied on a number fourteen hook,—white wings, peacock body with a belt of crimson silk,—and sent it out again, a foot farther up the stream and a shade closer to the weeds. As it settled on the water, there was a flash of gold from the shadow beneath the logs, and a quick turn of the wrist made the tiny hook fast in the fish. He fought wildly to get back to the shelter of his logs, but the four ounce rod had spring enough in it to hold him firmly away from that dangerous retreat. Then he splurged up and down the open water, and made fierce dashes among the grassy shallows, and seemed about to escape a dozen times. But at last his force was played out; he came slowly towards the boat, turning on his side, and I netted him in my hat.

"Bully for us;" said the boy, "we got him! What a dandy!"

It was indeed one of the handsomest fish that I have ever taken on the South Side,—just short of two pounds and a quarter,—small head, broad tail, and well-rounded sides coloured with orange and blue and gold and red. A pair of the same kind, one weighing two pounds and the other a pound and three quarters, were taken by careful fishing down the lower end of the pool, and then we rowed home through the dusk, pleasantly convinced that there is no virtue more certainly rewarded than the patience of anglers, and entirely willing to put up with a cold supper and a mild reproof for the sake of sport.

Of course we could not resist the temptation to show those fish to the neighbours. But, equally of course, we evaded the request to give precise information as to the precise place where they were caught. Indeed, I fear that there must have been something confused in our description of where we had been on that afternoon. Our carefully selected language may have been open to misunderstanding. At all events, the next day, which was the Sabbath, there was a row of eager but unprincipled anglers sitting on a bridge *over another stream*, and fishing for trout with worms and large expectations, but without visible results.

The boy and I agreed that if this did not teach a good moral lesson it was not our fault.

I obtained the boy's consent to admit the partner of my life's joys and two of our children to the secret of the brook, and thereafter, when we visited it, we took the fly-rod with us. If by chance another boat passed us in the estuary, we were never fishing, but only gathering flowers, or going for a picnic, or taking photographs. But when the uninitiated ones had passed by, we would get out the rod again, and try a few more casts.

One day in particular I remember, when Graygown and little Teddy were my companions. We really had no hopes of angling, for the hour was mid-noon, and the day was warm and still. But suddenly the trout, by one of those unaccountable freaks which make their disposition so interesting and attractive, began to rise all about us in a bend of the stream.

"Look!" said Teddy; "wherever you see one of those big smiles on the water, I believe there's a fish!"

Fortunately the rod was at hand. Graygown and Teddy managed the boat and the landing-net with consummate skill. We landed no less

than a dozen beautiful fish at that most un-
likely hour and then solemnly shook hands all
around.

There is a peculiar pleasure in doing a thing
like this, catching trout in a place where nobody
thinks of looking for them, and at an hour when
everybody believes they cannot be caught. It
is more fun to take one good fish out of an old,
fished-out stream, near at hand to the village,
than to fill a basket from some far-famed and
well-stocked water. It is the unexpected touch
that tickles our sense of pleasure. While life
lasts, we are always hoping for it and expecting
it. There is no country so civilized, no existence
so humdrum, that there is not room enough in
it somewhere for a lazy, idle brook, an encourager of indolence, with hope of happy surprises.

THE OPEN FIRE

"*It is a vulgar notion that a fire is only for heat. A chief value of it is, however, to look at. And it is never twice the same.*"—CHARLES DUDLEY WARNER: *Backlog Studies.*

THE OPEN FIRE

I

LIGHTING UP

MAN is the animal that has made friends with the fire.

All the other creatures, in their natural state, are afraid of it. They look upon it with wonder and dismay. It fascinates them, sometimes, with its glittering eyes in the night. The squirrels and the hares come pattering softly towards it through the underbrush around the new camp. The fascinated deer stares into the blaze of the jack-light while the hunter's canoe creeps through the lily-pads. But the charm that masters them is one of dread, not of love. It is the witchcraft of the serpent's lambent look. When they know what it means, when the heat of the fire touches them, or even when its smell comes clearly to their most delicate sense, they recognize it as their enemy, the Wild Huntsman whose red hounds can follow, follow for days without wearying, growing stronger and more furious with every turn of

215

the chase. Let but a trail of smoke drift down the wind across the forest, and all the game for miles and miles will catch the signal for fear and flight.

Many of the animals have learned how to make houses for themselves. The *cabane* of the beaver is a wonder of neatness and comfort, much preferable to the wigwam of his Indian hunter. The muskrat knows how thick and high to build the dome of his waterside cottage, in order to protect himself against the frost of the coming winter and the floods of the following spring. The woodchuck's house has two or three doors; and the squirrel's dwelling is provided with a good bed and a convenient storehouse for nuts and acorns. The sportive otters have a toboggan slide in front of their residence; and the moose in winter make a "yard," where they can take exercise comfortably and find shelter for sleep. But there is one thing lacking in all these various dwellings, —a fireplace.

Man is the only creature that dares to light a fire and to live with it. The reason? Because he alone has learned how to put it out.

It is true that two of his humbler friends have been converted to fire-worship. The dog and the cat, being half-humanized, have begun to love the fire. I suppose that a cat seldom comes so near to feeling a true sense of affection as when she has finished her saucer of bread and milk, and stretched herself luxuriously underneath the kitchen stove, while her faithful mistress washes up the dishes. As for a dog, I am sure that his admiring love for his master is never greater than when they come in together from the hunt, wet and tired, and the man gathers a pile of wood in front of the tent, touches it with a tiny magic wand, and suddenly the clear, consoling flame springs up, saying cheerfully, "Here we are, at home in the forest; come into the warmth; rest, and eat, and sleep." When the weary, shivering dog sees this miracle, he knows that his master is a great man and a lord of things.

After all, that is the only real open fire. Wood is the fuel for it. Out-of-doors is the place for it. A furnace is an underground prison for a toiling slave. A stove is a cage for a tame bird. Even a broad hearthstone and a pair of glittering andirons—the best ornament of a room—must be accepted as an imitation of the real thing. The veritable open fire is built in the open, with the whole earth for a fire place and the sky for a chimney.

To start a fire in the open is by no means as

easy as it looks. It is one of those simple tricks that every one thinks he can perform until he tries it.

To do it without trying,—accidentally and unwillingly,—that, of course, is a thing for which any fool is fit. You knock out the ashes from your pipe on a fallen log; you toss the end of a match into a patch of grass, green on top, but dry as punk underneath; you scatter the dead brands of an old fire among the moss,—a conflagration is under way before you know it.

A wood-fire in the open is one thing; a comfort and a joy. Fire in the woods is another thing; a terror, an uncontrollable fury, a burning shame.

But the lighting up of a proper fire, kindly, approachable, serviceable, docile, is a work of intelligence. If, perhaps, you have to do it in the rain, with a single match, it requires no little art and skill.

There is plenty of wood everywhere, but not a bit to burn. The fallen trees are waterlogged. The dead leaves are as damp as grief. The charred sticks that you find in an old fireplace are absolutely incombustible. Do not trust the handful of withered twigs and branches that you gather from the spruce-trees. They seem dry, but they are little better for your purpose than so much asbestos. You make a pile of them in some apparently suitable hollow, and lay a few larger sticks on top. Then you hastily scratch your solitary match on the seat of your trousers and thrust it into the pile of twigs. What happens? The wind whirls around in your stupid little hollow, and the blue flame of the sulphur spirts and sputters for an instant, and then goes out. Or perhaps there is a moment of stillness; the match flares up bravely; the nearest twigs catch fire, crackling and sparkling; you hurriedly lay on more sticks; but the fire deliberately dodges them, creeps to the corner of the pile where the twigs are fewest and dampest, snaps feebly a few times, and expires in smoke. Now where are you? How far is it to the nearest match?

If you are wise, you will always lay your fire before you light it. Time is never saved by doing a thing badly.

II

THE CAMP-FIRE

In the making of fires there is as much difference as in the building of houses. Everything depends upon the purpose that you have in view. There is the camp-fire, and the cooking-fire, and the smudge-fire, and the little friendship-fire,—not to speak of other minor varieties. Each of these has its own proper style of architecture, and to mix them is false art and poor economy.

The object of the camp-fire is to give heat, and incidentally light, to your tent or shanty. You can hardly build this kind of a fire unless you have a good axe and know how to chop. For the first thing that you need is a solid back-log, the thicker the better, to hold the heat and reflect it into the tent. This log must not be too dry, or it will burn out quickly. Neither must it be too damp, else it will smoulder and discourage the fire. The best wood for it is the body of a yellow birch, and, next to that, a green balsam. It should be five or six feet long, and at least two and a half feet in diameter. If you cannot find a tree thick enough, cut two or three lengths of a smaller one; lay the thickest log on the ground first, about ten or twelve feet in front of the tent; drive two strong stakes behind it, slanting a little backward; and lay the other logs on top of the first, resting against the stakes.

Now you are ready for the hand-chunks, or andirons. These are shorter sticks of wood, eight or ten inches thick, laid at right angles to the backlog, four or five feet apart. Across these you are to build up the firewood proper.

Use a dry spruce-tree, not one that has fallen, but one that is dead and still standing, if you want a lively, snapping fire. Use a hard maple or a hickory if you want a fire that will burn steadily and make few sparks. But if you like a fire to blaze up at first with a splendid flame, and then burn on with an enduring heat far into the night, a young white birch with the bark on is the tree to choose. Six or eight round sticks of this laid across the hand-chunks, with perhaps a few quarterings of a larger tree, will make a glorious fire.

But before you put these on, you must be ready to light up. A few splinters of dry spruce or pine or balsam, stood endwise against the backlog, or, better still, piled up in a pyramid between the hand-chunks; a few strips of birch-bark; and one good match,—these are all that you want. But be sure that your match is a good one. It is better to see to this before you go into the brush. Your comfort, even your life, may depend on it.

"*Avec ces allumettes-là*," said my guide at *Lac St. Jean* one day, as he vainly tried to light his pipe with a box of parlour matches from the hotel,—"*avec ces gnognottes d'allumettes on pourra mourir au bois!*"

In the woods, the old-fashioned brimstone match of our grandfathers—the match with a brown head and a stout stick and a dreadful smell—is the best. But if you have only one, do not trust even that to light your fire directly. Use it first to touch off a roll of birch-bark which you hold in your hand. Then, when the bark is well alight, crinkling and curling, push it under the heap of kindlings, give the flame time to take a good hold, and lay your wood over it, a stick at a time, until the whole pile is blazing. Now your fire is started. Your friendly little red-haired gnome is ready to serve you through the night.

He will dry your clothes if you are wet. He will cheer you up if you are despondent. He will diffuse an air of sociability through the camp, and draw the men together in a half circle for story-telling and jokes and singing. He will hold a flambeau for you while you spread your blankets on the boughs and dress for bed. He will keep you warm while you sleep,—at least till about three o'clock in the morning, when you dream that you are out sleighing in your pajamas, and wake up with a shiver.

"*Holà, Ferdinand, François!*" you call out

from your bed, pulling the blankets over your ears; "*Ramanchez le feu, s'il vous plait. C'est un freite de chien.*"

III

THE COOKING-FIRE

Of course such a fire as I have been describing can be used for cooking, when it has burned down a little, and there is a bed of hot embers in front of the backlog. But a correct kitchen fire should be constructed after another fashion. What you want now is not blaze, but heat, and that not diffused, but concentrated. You must be able to' get close to your fire without burning your boots or scorching your face.

If you have time and the material, make a fireplace of big stones. But not of granite, for that will split with the heat, and perhaps fly in your face.

If you are in a hurry and there are no suitable stones at hand, lay two good logs nearly parallel with each other, a foot or so apart, and build your fire between them. For a cooking-fire, use split wood in short sticks. Let the first supply burn to glowing coals before you begin. A frying-pan that is lukewarm one minute and red-hot the next is the abomination of desola-

223

tion. If you want black toast, have it made before a fresh, sputtering, blazing heap of wood.

In fires, as in men, an excess of energy is a lack of usefulness. The best work is done without many sparks. *Just enough* is the right kind of a fire and a feast.

To know how to cook is not a very elegant accomplishment. Yet there are times and seasons when it seems to come in better than familiarity with the dead languages, or much skill upon the lute.

You cannot always rely on your guides for a tasteful preparation of food. Many of them are ignorant of the difference between frying and broiling, and their notion of boiling a potato or a fish is to reduce it to a pulp. Now and then you find a man who has a natural inclination to the culinary art, and who does very well within familiar limits.

Old Edouard, the Montaignais Indian, who cooked for my friends H. E. G. and C. S. D. last summer on the *Ste. Marguérite en bas*, was such a man. But Edouard could not read, and the only way he could tell the nature of the canned provisions was by the pictures on the cans. If the picture was strange to him, there was no guessing what he would do with the contents of the can. He was capable of roasting strawberries, and serving green peas cold for dessert. One day a can of mullagatawny soup and a can of apricots were handed out to him simultaneously and without explanations. Edouard solved the problem by opening both cans and cooking them together. We had a new soup that day, *mullagatawny aux abricots*. It was not as bad as it sounds. It tasted somewhat like chutney.

The real reason why food that is cooked over an open fire tastes so good to us is because we are really hungry when we get it. The man who puts up provisions for camp has a great advantage over the dealers who must satisfy the pampered appetite of people in houses. I never can get any bacon in New York like that which I buy at a little shop in Quebec to take into the woods. If I ever set up in the grocery business, I shall try to get a good trade among anglers. It will be easy to please my customers.

The reputation that trout enjoy as a food-fish is partly due to the fact that they are usually cooked over an open fire. In the city they never taste as good. It is not merely a difference in freshness. It is a change in the sauce. If the truth must be told, even by an angler, there are at least five salt-water fish which are better than trout,—to eat. There is none better to catch.

IV

THE SMUDGE-FIRE

But enough of the cooking-fire. Let us turn now to the subject of the smudge, known in Lower Canada as *la boucane*. The smudge owes its existence to the pungent mosquito, the sanguinary black-fly, and the peppery midge,—*le maringouin, la moustique, et le brûlot*. To what it owes its English name I do not know; but its French name means simply a thick, nauseating, intolerable smoke.

The smudge is called into being for the express purpose of creating a smoke of this kind, which is as disagreeable to the mosquito, the black-fly, and the midge as it is to the man whom they are devouring. But the man survives the smoke, while the insects succumb to it, being destroyed or driven away. Therefore the smudge, dark and bitter in itself, frequently becomes, like adversity, sweet in its uses. It must be regarded as a form of fire with which man has made friends under the pressure of a cruel necessity.

It would seem as if it ought to be the simplest affair in the world to light up a smudge. And so it is—if you are not trying.

An attempt to produce almost any other kind

226

of a fire will bring forth smoke abundantly. But when you deliberately undertake to create a smudge, flames break from the wettest timber, and green moss blazes with a furious heat. You hastily gather handfuls of seemingly incombustible material and throw it on the fire, but the conflagration increases. Grass and green leaves hesitate for an instant and then flash up like tinder. The more you put on, the more your smudge rebels against its proper task of smudging. It makes a pleasant warmth to encourage the black-flies; and bright light to attract and cheer the mosquitoes. Your effort is a brilliant failure.

The proper way to make a smudge is this. Begin with a very little, lowly fire. Let it be bright, but not ambitious. Don't try to make a smoke yet.

Then gather a good supply of stuff which seems likely to suppress fire without smothering it. Moss of a certain kind will do, but not the soft, feathery moss that grows so deep among the spruce-trees. Half-decayed wood is good; spongy, moist, unpleasant stuff, a vegetable wet blanket. The bark of dead evergreen trees, hemlock, cedar, or balsam is better still. Gather a plentiful store of it. But don't try to make a smoke yet.

Let your fire burn a while longer; cheer it up

a little. Get some clear, resolute, unquench-
able coals aglow in the heart of it. Don't try
to make a smoke yet.

Now pile on your smouldering fuel. Fan it
with your hat. Kneel down and blow it, and
in ten minutes you will have a smoke that will
make you wish you had never been born.

That is the proper way to make a smudge.
But the easiest way is to ask your guide to make
it for you.

If he makes it in an old iron pot, so much
the better, for then you can move it around to
the windward when the breeze veers, and carry
it into your tent without risk of setting everything on fire, and even take it with you in the
canoe while you are fishing.

Some of the pleasantest pictures in the angler's
gallery of remembrance are framed in the smoke
that rises from a smudge.

With my eyes shut, I can call up a vision of
eight birch-bark canoes floating side by side on
Moosehead Lake, on a fair June morning, fifteen
years ago. They are anchored off Green Island,
riding easily on the long, gentle waves. In the
stern of each canoe there is a guide with a long-
handled net; in the bow, an angler with a light
fly-rod; in the middle, a smudge-kettle, smoking
steadily. In the air to the windward of the

little fleet hovers a swarm of flies drifting down on the shore breeze, with bloody purpose in their breasts, but baffled by the protecting smoke. In the water to the leeward plays a school of speckled trout, feeding on the minnows that hang around the sunken ledges of rock. As a larger wave than usual passes over the ledges, it lifts the fish up, and you can see the big fellows, three, and four, and even five pounds apiece, poising themselves in the clear brown water. A long cast will send the fly over one of them. Let it sink a foot. Draw it up with a fluttering motion. Now the fish sees it, and turns to catch it. There is a yellow gleam in the depth, a sudden swirl on the surface; you strike sharply, and the trout is matching his strength against the spring of your four ounces of split bamboo.

You can guess at his size, as he breaks water, by the breadth of his tail: a pound of weight to an inch of tail,—that is the traditional measure, and it usually comes pretty close to the mark, at least in the case of large fish. But it is never safe to record the weight until the trout is in the canoe. As the Canadian hunters say, "Sell not the skin of the bear while he carries it."

Now the breeze that blows over Green Island

drops away, and the smoke of the eight smudge-kettles falls like a thick curtain. The canoes, the dark shores of Norcross Point, the twin peaks of Spencer Mountain, the dim blue summit of Katahdin, the dazzling sapphire sky, the flocks of fleece-white clouds shepherded on high by the western wind, all have vanished. With closed eyes I see another vision, still framed in smoke,—a vision of yesterday.

It is a wild river flowing into the Gulf of St. Lawrence, on the *Côte Nord*, far down towards Labrador. There is a long, narrow, swift pool between two parallel ridges of rock. Over the ridge on the right pours a cataract of pale yellow foam. At the bottom of the pool, the water slides down into a furious rapid, and dashes straight through an impassable gorge half a mile to the sea. The pool is full of salmon, leaping merrily in their delight at coming into their native stream. The air is full of black-flies, rejoicing in the warmth of the July sun. On a slippery point of rock, below the fall, are two anglers, tempting the fish and enduring the flies. Behind them is an old *habitant* raising a mighty column of smoke.

Through the cloudy pillar which keeps back the Egyptian host, you see the waving of a long rod. A silver-gray fly with a barbed tail darts out across the pool, swings around with the current, well under water, and slowly works past the big rock in the centre, just at the head of the rapid. Almost past it, but not quite: for suddenly the fly disappears; the line begins to run out; the reel sings sharp and shrill; a salmon is hooked.

But how well is he hooked? That is the question. This is no easy pool to play a fish in. There is no chance to jump into a canoe and drop below him, and get the current to help you in drowning him. You cannot follow him along the shore. You cannot even lead him into quiet water, where the gaffer can creep near to him unseen and drag him in with a quick stroke. You must fight your fish to a finish, and all the advantages are on his side. The current is terribly strong. If he makes up his mind to go downstream to the sea, the only thing you can do is to hold him by main force; and then it is ten to one that the hook tears out or the leader breaks.

It is not in human nature for one man to watch another handling a fish in such a place without giving advice. "Keep the tip of your rod up. Don't let your reel overrun. Stir him up a little, he's sulking. Don't let him 'jig,' or you'll lose him. You're playing him too hard. There, he's going to jump again. Drop your tip. Stop him, quick! he's going down the rapid!"

Of course the man who is playing the salmon does not like this. If he is quick-tempered, sooner or later he tells his counsellor to shut up. But if he is a gentle, early-Christian kind of a man, wise as a serpent and harmless as a dove, he follows the advice that is given to him, promptly and exactly. Then, when it is all ended, and he has seen the big fish, with the line over his shoulder, poised for an instant on the crest of the first billow of the rapid, and has felt the leader stretch and give and *snap!*—then he can have the satisfaction, while he reels in his slack line, of saying to his friend, "Well, old man, I did everything just as you told me. But I think if I had pushed that fish a little harder at the beginning, *as I wanted to*, I might have saved him."

But really, of course, the chances were all against it. In such a pool, most of the larger fish get away. Their weight gives them a tremendous pull. The fish that are stopped from going into the rapid, and dragged back from the curling wave, are usually the smaller ones. Here they are,—twelve pounds, eight pounds, six pounds, five pounds and a half, *four pounds!*

THE OPEN FIRE

Is not this the smallest salmon that you ever saw? Not a grilse, you understand, but a real salmon, of brightest silver, hall-marked with St. Andrew's cross.

Now let us sit down for a moment and watch the fish trying to leap up the falls. There is a clear jump of about ten feet, and above that an apparently impossible climb of ten feet more up a ladder of twisting foam. A salmon darts from the boiling water at the bottom of the fall like an arrow from a bow. He rises in a beautiful curve, fins laid close to his body and tail quivering; but he has miscalculated his distance. He is on the downward curve when the water strikes him and tumbles him back. A bold little trout, not more than eighteen inches long, makes a jump at the side of the fall, where the water is thin, and is rolled over and over in the spray. A larger salmon rises close beside us with a tremendous rush, bumps his nose against a jutting rock, and flops back into the pool. Now comes a fish who has made his calculations exactly. He leaves the pool about eight feet from the foot of the fall, rises swiftly, spreads his fins, and curves his tail as if he were flying, strikes the water where it is thickest just below the brink, holds on desperately, and drives himself, with one last wriggle, through the bend-ing stream, over the edge, and up the first step of the foaming stairway. He has obeyed the strongest instinct of his nature, and gone up to make love in the highest fresh water that he can reach.

The smoke of the smudge-fire is sharp and tearful, but a man can learn to endure a good deal of it when he can look through its rings at such scenes as these.

V

THE LITTLE FRIENDSHIP-FIRE

There are times and seasons when the angler has no need of any of the three fires of which we have been talking. He sleeps in a house. His breakfast and dinner are cooked for him in a kitchen. He is in no great danger from black-flies or mosquitoes. All he needs now, as he sets out to spend a day on the Neversink, or the Willowemoc, or the Shepaug, or the Swiftwater, is a good lunch in his pocket, and a little friendship-fire to burn pleasantly beside him while he eats his frugal fare and prolongs his noonday rest.

This form of fire does less work than any other in the world. Yet it is far from being useless; and I, for one, should be sorry to live without it. Its only use is to make a visible centre of interest where there are two or three anglers eating their lunch together, or to supply a kind of companionship to a lone fisherman. It is kindled and burns for no other purpose than to give you the sense of being at home and at ease. Why the fire should do this, I cannot tell, but it does.

You may build your friendship-fire in almost any way that pleases you; but this is the way in which you shall build it best. You have no axe, of course, so you must look about for the driest sticks that you can find. Do not seek them close beside the stream, for there they are likely to be water-soaked; but go back into the woods a bit and gather a good armful of fuel. Then break it, if you can, into lengths of about two feet, and construct your fire in the following fashion.

Lay two sticks parallel, and put between them a pile of dried grass, dead leaves, small twigs, and the paper in which your lunch was wrapped. Then lay two other sticks crosswise on top of your first pair. Strike your match and touch your kindlings. As the fire catches, lay on other pairs of sticks, each pair crosswise to the pair that is below it, until you have a pyramid of flame. This is "a Micmac fire" such as the Indians make in the woods.

FISHERMAN'S LUCK

Now you can pull off your wading-boots and warm your feet at the blaze. You can toast your bread if you like. You can even make shift to broil one of your trout, fastened on the end of a birch twig if you have a fancy that way. When your hunger is satisfied, you shake out the crumbs for the birds and the squirrels, pick up a stick with a coal at the end to light your pipe, put some more wood on your fire, and settle down for an hour's reading if you have a book in your pocket, or for a good talk if you have a comrade with you.

The stream of time flows swift and smooth, by such a fire as this. The moments slip past unheeded; the sun sinks down his western arch; the shadows begin to fall across the brook; it is time to move on for the afternoon fishing. The fire has almost burned out. But do not trust it too much. Throw some sand over it, or bring a hatful of water from the brook to pour on it, until you are sure that the last glowing ember is extinguished, and nothing but the black coals and the charred ends of the sticks are left.

Even the little friendship-fire must keep the law of the bush. All lights out when their purpose is fulfilled!

236

THE OPEN FIRE

VI

It is a question that we have often debated, in the informal meetings of our Petrine Club: Which is pleasanter,—to fish an old stream, or a new one?

The younger members are all for the "fresh woods and pastures new." They speak of the delight of turning off from the high-road into some faintly-marked trail; following it blindly through the forest, not knowing how far you have to go; hearing the voice of waters sounding through the woodland; leaving the path impatiently and striking straight across the underbrush; scrambling down a steep bank, pushing through a thicket of alders, and coming out suddenly, face to face with a beautiful, strange brook. It reminds you, of course, of some old friend. It is a little like the Beaverkill, or the Ausable, or the Gale River. And yet it is different. Every stream has its own character and disposition. Your new acquaintance invites you to a day of discoveries. If the water is high, you will follow it down, and have easy fishing. If the water is low, you will go upstream, and fish "fine and far-off." Every turn in the avenue which the little river has made for you opens up a new view,— a rocky gorge where the deep pools are divided by white-footed falls; a lofty forest where the shadows are deep and the trees arch overhead; a flat, sunny stretch where the stream is spread out, and pebbly islands divide the channels, and the big fish are lurking at the sides in the sheltered corners under the bushes. From scene to scene you follow on, delighted and expectant, until the night suddenly drops its veil, and then you will be lucky if you can find your way home in the dark!

Yes, it is all very good, this exploration of new streams. But, for my part, I like still better to go back to a familiar little river, and fish or dream along the banks where I have dreamed and fished before. I know every bend and curve: the sharp turn where the water runs under the roots of the old hemlock-tree; the snaky glen, where the alders stretch their arms far out across the stream; the meadow reach, where the trout are fat and silvery, and will only rise about sunrise or sundown, unless the day is cloudy; the Naiad's Elbow, where the brook rounds itself, smooth and dimpled, to embrace a cluster of pink laurel-bushes. All these I know; yes, and almost every current and eddy and backwater I know long before I come to it. I remember where I caught the big trout the first year I came to the stream; and where I lost a bigger one. I remember the pool where there were plenty of good fish last year, and wonder whether they are there now.

Better things than these I remember: the companions with whom I have followed the stream in days long past; the rendezvous with a comrade at the place where the rustic bridge crosses the brook; the hours of sweet converse beside the friendship-fire; the meeting at twilight with my lady Graygown and the children who have come down by the wood-road to walk home with me.

Surely it is pleasant to follow an old stream. Flowers grow along its banks which are not to be found anywhere else in the wide world. "There is rosemary, that's for remembrance; and there is pansies, that's for thoughts!"

One May evening, a couple of years since, I was angling in the Swiftwater, and came upon Joseph Jefferson, stretched out on a large rock in midstream, and casting the fly down a long pool. He had passed the threescore years and ten, but he was as eager and as happy as a boy in his fishing.

"You here!" I cried. "What good fortune brought you into these waters?"

"Ah," he answered, "I fished this brook forty-five years ago. It was in the Paradise Valley that I first thought of Rip Van Winkle. I wanted to come back again for the sake of old times."

But what has all this to do with an open fire? I will tell you. It is at the places along the stream, where the little flames of love and friendship have been kindled in bygone days, that the past returns most vividly. These are the altars of remembrance.

It is strange how long a small fire will leave its mark. The charred sticks, the black coals, do not decay easily. If they lie well up the bank, out of reach of the spring floods, they will stay there for years. If you have chanced to build a rough fireplace of stones from the brook, it seems almost as if it would last forever.

There is a mossy knoll beneath a great butternut-tree on the Swiftwater where such a fireplace was built four years ago; and whenever I come to that place now I lay the rod aside, and sit down for a little while by the fast-flowing water, and remember.

This is what I see: A man wading up the stream, with a creel over his shoulder, and per-

haps a dozen trout in it; two little lads in gray
corduroys running down the path through the
woods to meet him, one carrying a frying-pan
and a kettle, the other with a basket of lunch on
his arm. Then I see the bright flames leaping
up in the fireplace, and hear the trout sizzling
in the pan, and smell the appetizing odour.
Now I see the lads coming back across the foot-
bridge that spans the stream, with a bottle of
milk from the nearest farmhouse. They are
laughing and teetering as they balance along
the single plank. Now the table is spread on
the moss. How good the lunch tastes ! Never
were there such pink-fleshed trout, such crisp
and savoury slices of broiled bacon. Douglas,
(the beloved doll that the younger lad shame-
facedly brings out from the pocket of his jacket,)
must certainly have some of it. And after the
lunch is finished, and the bird's portion has been
scattered on the moss, we creep carefully on our
hands and knees to the edge of the brook, and
look over the bank at the big trout that is poising himself in the amber water. We have tried
a dozen times to catch him, but never succeeded.
The next time, perhaps——

Well, the fireplace is still standing. The butternut-tree spreads its broad branches above the
stream. The violets and the bishop's-caps and

the wild anemones are sprinkled over the banks. The yellow-throat and the water-thrush and the vireos still sing the same tunes in the thicket. And the elder of the two lads often comes back with me to that pleasant place and shares my fisherman's luck beside the Swiftwater.

But the younger lad?

Ah, my little Barney, you have gone to follow a new stream,—clear as crystal,—flowing through fields of wonderful flowers that never fade. It is a strange river to Teddy and me; strange and very far away. Some day we shall see it with you; and you will teach us the names of those blossoms that do not wither. But till then, little Barney, the other lad and I will follow the old stream that flows by the woodland fireplace,—your altar.

Rue grows here. Yes, there is plenty of rue. But there is also rosemary, that's for remembrance! And close beside it I see a little heart's-ease.

242

"LITTLE BOATIE"

"LITTLE BOATIE"

A SLUMBER–SONG

FOR THE FISHERMAN'S CHILD

FURL your sail, my little boatie;
　　Here 's the haven still and deep,
Where the dreaming tides in-streaming
　　　　Up the channel creep.
Now the sunset breeze is dying;
Hear the plover, landward flying,
Softly down the twilight crying;
　　　Come to anchor, little boatie,
　　　　In the port of Sleep.

Far away, my little boatie,
　　Roaring waves are white with foam;
Ships are striving, onward driving,
　　　　Day and night they roam.
Father 's at the deep-sea trawling,
In the darkness, rowing, hauling,
While the hungry winds are calling,—
　　　God protect him, little boatie,
　　　　Bring him safely home!

FISHERMAN'S LUCK

Not for you, my little boatie,
    Is the wide and weary sea;
You 're too slender, and too tender,
    You must bide with me.
All day long you have been straying
Up and down the shore and playing;
Come to harbour, no delaying!
    Day is over, little boatie,
    Night falls suddenly.

Furl your sail, my little boatie;
    Fold your wings, my weary dove.
Dews are sprinkling, stars are twinkling
    Drowsily above.
Cease from sailing, cease from rowing;
Rock upon the dream-tide, knowing
Safely o'er your rest are glowing,
    All the night, my little boatie,
    Harbour-lights of love.

INDEX

INDEX

Adam: his early education, 87; his opinion of woman, 112.
"Afghan's Knife, The," 173.
Algebra: the equation of life, 12.
"Alice Lorraine," 150.
"Along New England Roads," 147.
Altars of remembrance, 240.
"Amateur Angler's Days in Dove Dale, An," 37, 145.
"American Angler's Book, The," 146.
"American Salmon Angler, The," 147.
"Among New England Hills," 147.
"Angler, The Compleat." See Walton, Izaak.
Angler: the education of an, 113.
"Angler's Guide, The," 141.
Angling: an affair of luck, 5; a means of escape from *tædium vitæ*, 13; books about, classified, 139, 140.
"Angling Reminiscences" of Thomas Tod Stoddart, 143.
"Angling Sketches," by Andrew Lang, 146.
Antony: deceived by Cleopatra, 148.
Arden, the Forest of: direction for reaching, 14.
Ascension Day: good for fishing, 6.

Bald Mountains, 183.
Banquets: two delectable ones, 19-21.

Baptists, Seventh-Day: an inducement to join them, 6.
Barber: the philosophic conduct of a, 16.
Barker, Thomas, 140.
Bartlett, Mr. John: piscatorial collection of, 139.
Bergen: town of, 166.
Berries, 77; Izaak Walton quoted on, 78.
Bethune, Rev. Dr. George W., an editor of Walton, 147.
Birds: their unexpectedness, 22; their courage, 24, 202; their manner of singing, 56-59, 75.
Birds named:
  Blue jay, 197.
  Boblink, 74.
  Brown thrush, 58.
  Catbird, 97, 197.
  Crow, 202.
  English sparrow, not a bird, 57, 99.
  Grosbeak, rose-breasted, 58.
  Hooded warbler, 23.
  Kingbird, 202.
  Mockingbird, 58.
  Oriole, 58.
  Parrot, 57.
  Partridge, 24.
  Pigeon-hawk, 181.
  Redstart, 23.
  Robin, 58.
  Rose-breasted grosbeak, 58.
  Spotted sandpiper, 25.
  Swallow, 182.

249

INDEX

Thrush, 182.
Veery, 58.
Vireos, 242.
Water-thrush, 242.
White-throat, 58.
Wood thrush, 58.
Wren, 58.
Yellow-throat, 181, 242.
Yellow warblers, 97.
Black, William: his knowledge of angling, 151.
Blackmore, R. D., 146; fishing described by, 150.
"Book of the Black Bass," 147.
Burgund: church at, 166.
Boyle, Hon. Robert, 144.
Brogue: as an ornament of speech, 69.
Brook: a lazy, idle, 193; in the bower, 194; considered as a sign, 198; the lesson of a, 203; fishing in a, 207.
Browsing: a diversion for anglers, 76.
Burroughs, John, 138.
Butler, Dr. William: his pleasant saying about the strawberry, 79; his character as a physician and a philosopher, 79–80.
"By Meadow and Stream," 145.
Byron, Lord: a detractor of Walton, 136.

Camp-fire: the art of kindling a, 220.
Camping: pleasures of, 17.
Cannon Mountain, 183.
"Chalk-Stream Studies," 144.
Chance: a good word with a bad reputation, 11.
Chatto, William Andrew, 130, 146.
Cheerfulness: a virtue in good talk, 70.

Christian character: illustrated, 30.
Civilization: a nervous disease, 199.
Cleopatra, 148.
"Cloister and the Hearth, The," 104.
Colquhoun, John, 142.
Conversation: compared with talk, 13.
Cook: a good, 224.
Cooking-fire: the art of kindling a, 223.
Cotton, Charles, 51, 140.
Crinkle-root, 77.
"Crocker's Hole," 146.
Crosby, Chancellor Howard: a good talker, 64.

Davy, Sir Humphry: slighted by Christopher North, 143.
"Days in Clover," 145.
Days: Superstitions about them, 6.
Dennys, John: "The Secrets of Angling," quoted, 137.
DePeyster, Mr. and Mrs.: the success of, in the art of the angler, 113.
DeQuincey, Thomas, 139.
Deucalion: the first artistic fisherman, 5.
Dickinson, Emily: quoted, 86.
Drivstuen, 173.

Eagle Cliff, 183.
Elizabeth, Queen, 80.
Elk: the Tarn of the, 172.
Emerson, Ralph Waldo: quoted, 106.
English sparrows: beasts, not birds, 57.

INDEX

"Essays Critical and Imaginative" of Christopher North, 143.
Etnadal, 164.
"Ettrick Shepherd," the, 51.

Fagernaes, 167.
Faleide, 170.
Fawkes, Guy, 80.
Fire: fear of animals of, 215; kindling a fire in the woods, 217; the camp-fire, 219; the cooking-fire, 223; the smudge-fire, 226; the little friendship-fire, 234.
Fish: their waywardness, 42, 211; how an angler feels about them, 26; whether they can hear, 51–53; domesticated, 88.
Fish named:
  Grass-pike, 205.
  Grayling, 50, 175.
  Grilse, 233.
  Ouananiche, 36, 37, 42, 43.
  Pickerel, 132.
  Pike, 11, 88.
  Salmon, 30, 36, 233.
  Sunfish, 205.
  Trout, 51, 53, 140, 150, 167, 175, 205, 209, 211, 225, 229.
"Fishin' Jimmy," 147.
Fishing: *passim*; an affair of luck, 5; lucky days for, 6; a means of escape from routine, 13; the only eventful mode of life, 13; good luck in, deserving of gratitude, 27; the schooling of a woman angler, 114; catching pickerel through the ice, 132; the best winter diversion indoors, 135; books on, 139–141; fish and fishing, 146; in old streams and new, 236.

"Fish-Tails and a Few Others," 145.
Flies: various theories for the use of, 42; the grasshopper a last hope, 43; style in, 140.
Flowers: wild and tame, 84; luck in finding, 86.
Flowers named:
  Anemone, 242.
  Anemone, double rue, 86.
  Bishop's-cap, 241.
  Gentian, fringed, 86.
  Hare-bells, 75.
  Heart's-ease, 242.
  Laurel, mountain, 75.
  Loose-strife, yellow, 75.
  Orchid, purple-fringed, 75.
  Prince's pine, 75.
  Rosemary, 239, 242.
  Rue, 242.
  Twin-flower, 76.
  Violet, 241.
"Fly-Fisher's Entomology, The," 53.
"Fly-Rods and Fly-Tackle," 147.
Fontainebleau, 88.
Forester, Frank, 146.
Forests: real and artificial, 89.
Fox: red, 197.
Franck, Richard: a detractor of Walton, 136.
Franconia Mountains, 182.
Freedom of spirit: an essential of good company, 67.
"Fresh Woods," 145.
Friendliness: its magical power, 71.
Friendship-fire, the little, 234.

Gambling: a harmless variety of, 10.
"Game Fish of the North," 147.
Garfield, Mount, 183.

251

INDEX

252

INDEX

INDEX

Rabbit: cotton-tail, 197.
"Rambles with a Fishing-Rod,"
  of E. S. Roscoe, 145.
Randsfjord, 160.
Raphael, the Archangel: his one-
  sided affability, 56.
Rauma: the vale of the, 175.
"Recreations of Christopher North,
  The," 143.
"Redgauntlet": angling in, 149.
Remembrance: altars of, 240.
"Rip Van Winkle," 103, 240.
"Rise of Silas Lapham, The," 104.
Ristigouche, 25.
"Rivals, The," 103.
Rivers, named:
  Ausable, 237.
  Baegna, 164.
  Bouquet, 169.
  Dove, 31.
  Gale, 182, 237.
  Hudson, 84.
  Lea, 31.
  Marshpee, 51.
  Meacham, 115.
  Metabetchouan, 71.
  Moose, 116.
  Naeselv, 167.
  Natasheebo, 126.
  Neversink, 234.
  New, 31.
  Penobscot, 169.
  P'tit Saguenay, 28.
  Randsfjord, 160.
  Rauma, 175.
  Ristigouche, 25.
  Saguenay, 29, 30.
  Shepaug, 234.
  Swiftwater, 75, 87, 234, 239,
    240, 242.
  Ulvaa, 175.
  Willowemoc, 234.

Rob Roy: an eel named, 52.
"Rod in India, The," 145.
"Romola," 104.
Romsdal, The, 166, 174.
Ronalds, Mr.: quoted, 53.
Roosevelt, Mr. Robert B., 147.
Roscoe, E. S., 145.
"Roundabout Papers," 59.

Sabbath-Day Point, 9.
Sage, Mr. Dean: piscatorial li-
  brary of, 139.
Saguenay, the Big, 29, 30.
Saguenay, the Little, 28.
Salmon, 27, 51.
"Salmonia," 143.
"Schuylkill Fishing Company,"
  146.
Scott, Sir Walter: quoted, 149.
Sermon: a good one, 50.
Singlewitz, Solomon: quoted, 112,
  156.
"Sketch Book," 152.
Skogstad: the station at, 168.
Skydsgut, 163.
Slosson, Mrs. Annie Trumbull:
  her "Fishin' Jimmy," 147.
Smallness: not a mark of inferi-
  ority, 83.
Smith, Captain John, 82.
Smudge; the art of kindling a,
  226.
Spearmint, 77.
St. Anthony of Padua, 50.
St. Brandan, 50.
St. Francis of Assisi, 19.
St. Peter, 12, 28.
Stedman, Mr. Edmund Clarence,
  141.
Steele, Richard: quoted, 106.
Stevenson, Robert Louis: quoted,
  54, 190.

254

INDEX

Stoddart, Thomas Tod, 142.
Stolkjaerres, 166.
Storm King Club: a festival of, 84.
Strawberry, the: one that God made, 78; imputed to England, 80; wild and tame, 83.
Stuefloten, 174, 175.
Style: the value of, 83.
Summer Schools: persons for whom they have no attractions, 9.
Sunday: fishing on, 6.
"Superior Fishing," 147.
Swiftwater: a well-named brook, 75.

Talk: anglers urged to, 49–51; varieties of, 58–62; obstacles to its perfection, 63, 67, 68.
Talkability: defined, 54, 55; a talkable person, 56; contrasted with talkativity, 58; not the same as eloquence, 58; commended, 60–72; the fourfold conditions of, 63; goodness, 63; freedom, 67; gayety, 70; friendship, 71.
Tarn of the Elk, the, 172; trout in, 173.
Telephone: its influence on manners, 4.
Tennyson: as a talker, 68; quoted, 53.
Tent: life in a, 15.
Thackeray, W. M.: quoted, 59.
Thersites: as a journalist, 66.
Thomas, H. S., 145.
"Three Musketeers, The," 104, 173.
Timoleon: the unlucky one, 29.

Tobias, the son of Tobit: his adventure with a pike, 88.
Tommy's Rock: a good place for blackfish, 7.
"Treasure Island," 173.
Trees: why boys and girls love them, 87.
Trench, Archbishop, 200.
Trolley-car: the blessings of its absence, 18.
Trout, 51, 53, 150, 167, 206, 211, 256; taste of, for flies, 140; in Norway, 167; in the Tarn of the Elk, 173; in the Rauma in Norway, 175; a good catch, 209; eating vs. catching, 225.
Twin Mountain, 183.

Vacations: can be taken without long journeys, 14.
Valders, the vale of, 164, 176.
Vergil: quoted, 141.
Virginia: talk in, 69; its strawberries, 80, 82; bread in a Virginia country house, 174.

Walton, Izaak: described, 29, 30; quoted, 30, 78; his luck in literature, 135; his detractors, 136; Dr. Bethune's edition of, 147; fishermen born, not made, 147.
Warner, Charles Dudley: quoted, 214.
Water: emblem of instability, 8.
Weather: a subject of talk, 55, 61; various remarks on, 15–17, 90.
Webster, Daniel: as an angler, 51.
Wells, Mr. Henry P., 53, 147.
Wife: the right kind of a, 72.
Wilson, Professor John, "M. A." and "F. R. S.," 143.
"Winter's Tale, A," 103.

255

INDEX